BY THE SAME AUTHOR

How to Skin a Cat
Bauhinia Star
Knowing Me Roger Vim
The Redemption of Garry Jones
Perverse Consequences
Blink
Clydebank Blitz

Copyright © 2016 by Robert Blain

ISBN 9-781549-742538

1
=====

KISS IN A CLOSE

1960, Glasgow, Scotland...

The pair got off the Drumchapel tram just as an icy gust of wind blew up Govanhill Street. A pale late-afternoon sun slanted weakly through the tenements – warming the tarmac not one jot. The woman gave a laugh of delight at the shock of the chill. They dashed across the street for the relative shelter of the nearby opening of one of the apartment blocks. A cold wind swirled around the mouth of the close. She drew her shawl about her shoulders and shivered. The man took off his thick, warm coat and draped it around her, buttoning it from bottom to top so his hands fumbled with the final clasp as they pressed against her chest.

Briefly neither said anything, drinking in the significance of the moment. The tram rattled and grumbled away, bells dinging to alert pedestrians. Jude sucked down air in short bursts – breathless from the dash across the street and the proximity of the handsome stranger. He drew back slightly and smiled. She hesitated, staring back into his eyes like a startled deer. She adored the dashing figure he cut – his trilby set at a jaunty angle, a scarlet red cravat at his throat – an affirmation of life in the grey of the city.

'I'd like to take you for a ride in my motor car, Jude. You deserve better than being dragged about on a sodding tram like the hoi polloi.'

The "deserve better" hung in the air, a reference – they both knew – to her husband.

She took off her hat and shook out her auburn hair. It was a gesture of theatre, true to the actress she was, to allow her a little time to regain her composure and show Colin that she was not overawed by his presence. She had what Glaswegians call "the gallus" a kind of unconquerable spirit, a haughtiness. Cock o' the walk. He put his hand to his own hat, but left it in place, acutely conscious of his receding hairline.

'Trams are getting phased out. They're all going to be decommissioned and sent to Hong Kong,' he continued. 'Bloody daft idea in a city as dreich as Glasgow anyway.'

'I'd like a ride in your car very much,' she finally replied.

'I'd like that just fine too, Judith Baxter. '

'You don't need to be so formal Colin. '

'My coat looks just grand on you,' he managed in a low whisper.

He put his hands on her shoulders and rubbed them, as if trying to warm her up. He put his mouth to her ear.

'He must be soft in the heid to encourage me to spend time with a woman like you.'

Colin's use of the word "heid" was a rare foray into the Glasgow vernacular – so unlike her gruff, working-class husband, Jude thought, who seemed to revel in his humble origins. Colin's turn of phrase was what most Glaswegians

4

would call plummy, or put on. But so what? At least he had designs on something better. But she said nothing, just closed her eyes and leant back ever so slightly against the wall. She felt herself trembling.

As he kissed her, her lips parted easily. At first there was relief, relief they were finally doing it. Then she was lost in the moment. Colin broke off suddenly as someone entered the close – a workman in dungarees, returning from a day's toil. He eyed the pair briefly and continued on his way up the stairs, whistling Danny Boy as he went.

'Thank Christ that wasn't one of the neighbours,' hissed Jude. 'Colin, we've got to stop before someone recognises us.'

But immediately belying this she took him in her arms and began kissing him again. She felt him smiling under his lips but she pressed on until he responded.

She was thrilled. The thrill of the chase. The thrill of getting her man. But most of all was the thrill of being such a naughty girl. Her mother would be appalled. It was delicious; there was no way her mammy was going to make her feel guilty. Not this time. She put her hand up under the back of his trilby and stroked his hair. He tightened his grip around her waist. They kissed, and kissed, and kissed.

2

=====

SOUTHPAW

Jimmy Baxter stumbled but kept his feet. The right hook from his opponent had left him shaken. If he hadn't feinted just before impact, he would have been caught flush and on the canvas. Still, Baxter's ears were ringing. Momentarily the ring went dark. The younger man shuffled on the spot and banged his gloves together to egg himself on. Sensing blood, he went in for the kill. Swinging a right, a left, another right. Baxter raised his arms – more muscle memory than technique – and the blows thudded into his body. His southpaw stance had saved him – confounding his rival and denying him a clean headshot.

Beyond the confines of the Glasgow Green gym, mist rolled off the icy Clyde River and blanketed the surrounds in a chilly damp. But in the ring the two opponents were sheened in sweat, bare except for black boxer shorts and boots. The younger man was wiry and taller, with a superior reach. But the 38-year-old Baxter was blessed with a sculpted boxer's physique. He shook his head in an attempt to regain focus. A bead of sweat flicked off his mop of dark, curly hair.

'C'mon Frankie, finish him off!' shouted the trainer.

But the young gun was too winded from his effort to respond

immediately. He sucked in a couple of deep breaths.

The sharp words also revived Baxter. In the breathing space, he began to summon his anger – he was going to need it. He had learned to fight at school to silence those who called him "bastard". It was a stigma he couldn't shake. The taunt never stopped ringing in his ears, even in adulthood. The rage of having never known his father made him a formidable opponent, even when fighting a much younger man. But Baxter was having an off night, something that was happening more and more the deeper he progressed into his thirties. He knew he was going to have to give the game away. But not now. Not this night.

He had a trick to fire himself up when he needed an extra push. It was a review of his sporting prowess as a footballer for Stanley Celtic – perversely a Protestant team – by a journalist from *The Glasgow Herald*. The scribe had turned up and the same day a talent scout had come to the match to watch the young Baxter play. Parts of the journalist's article, which circulated the length and breadth of Glasgow on the Saturday evening edition, were etched on his soul – still a burning source of humiliation years later…

'Baxter was put through with the prince of passes…'
The young man got his second wind and set upon Baxter with a quick left-and-right combination that Baxter took on the body.

'…The goalmouth yawned like the Glasgow Tunnel…'
The young fighter threw a haymaker. Baxter ducked, throwing Frankie off guard. As he overbalanced, Baxter connected with a short left jab.

'…Then with the back of the net beckoning…'
Stung by this unexpected turn of events, Frankie unleashed a barrage of blows that Baxter again took on the body. As his

opponent paused for breath, Baxter hit him with a right hook that connected with a thud. Frankie eyed Baxter with surprise, as if he had somehow come back from the dead. What angered Baxter most was that he was two-footed. He could have, *should* have, smashed the ball into the back of the net with either peg. That would have shut the journalist up for good.

'*...Baxter poked it meekly into the goalkeeper's hands...*' Baxter followed up quickly with a right and left combination and Frankie swayed and dropped onto one knee. A white cotton towel fluttered into the ring.

'Aye, that'll do Frankie,' said the trainer. 'I want to keep you in shape for the juniors next week, no copping a hiding from a man twice your age.'

Frankie stood up. The two fighters acknowledged each other with a nod and returned to their corners. Baxter took three prolonged breaths and exhaled deeply. He had roused himself to a near frenzy and was now trying to come back down. The face of the sports journalist was slowly fading.

'I wish I'd had you as an eighteen year old, Jimmy Baxter,' said the trainer.

Baxter nodded curtly at the compliment. Then he slung a towel over his sweat-soaked torso and headed for the showers.

As he left the ring, two men he hadn't noticed previously approached. One he recognised, Willie Boyd – a former colleague. The other was smaller and darker, almost of Spanish appearance. Baxter had never met him before but he had an inkling of who he might be.

'It's been a while,' said Willie. 'How are things working out for you?'

'Aye, no bad,' said Baxter.

'I'd like you to meet my boss,' said Willie. 'Alec McManus.'

Baxter's suspicions were confirmed. Alec McManus. Or "Wee Alec" as he was known around the traps. A noted hard-man, fast building a reputation as one of the most feared gang leaders in Glasgow.

Wee Alec nodded at Baxter but did not extend his hand. Their eyes met. Baxter experienced a worm of unease as he held the gang leader's cold, intense gaze. Wee Alec's reputation for viciousness was revealed in those dead eyes, right now sizing him up.

'I've got a proposal for you,' said Wee Alec. 'I'm looking for a boxer.'

Wee Alec had the look of a Catalan about him but his Glasgow twang was unmistakable – a sharp Gorbals bite, a relic of the place he was raised. There were rumours that his father was of Mediterranean descent, not that anyone would dare say that to his face.

'We can make it well worth your while,' chimed in Willie.

'I'm too old to take up boxing seriously,' said Baxter. 'You should consider someone younger.'

The eyes of the three men wandered over to Frankie, still sitting in his corner of the ring after the bout, dabbing sweat off his face with a towel.

'I want a man who can box,' said Wee Alec. 'No a pretty boy. Think about it Jimmy Baxter. Will you do that for me?'

'Oh aye. '

'Good man. We'll be in touch.'

The two men nodded in Baxter's direction and left as suddenly as they had appeared.

Baxter continued on towards the showers. He was somewhat

flattered by Wee Alec's interest in him but he had no intention of taking him up on the offer. He didn't know exactly what the gang leader's "proposal" was going to entail but he doubted it was honourable – taking a fall probably. No, he had no desire to box for Wee Alec, or anyone else for that matter.

Sometimes Baxter wondered if he had chosen the wrong sport. Surely a celebrated football career had once beckoned. What if he hadn't fluffed his chances in front of the talent scout all those years ago? But sporting glory eluded him – at least as a boxer – because deep down, Jimmy Baxter despised violence.

3

=====

THE VIAL

Present day, Melbourne, Australia...

Just for the record, I am the fourth member of the Baxter clan, born after the family left Govanhill Street. I came nine years after the third sibling. Admittedly that's quite a gap. Although my mother was fond of saying that I was the only one of her children who *was* planned. That comment has often made me stop and wonder.

*****

Buddy Holly. The great unrealised American musical talent of his time. Who could have been anything. Whose potential was tragically cut short on an ill-fated plane ride in a February snowstorm all those years ago. Buddy Holly, who, at the same age as Lennon and McCartney, Jagger and Richards, was writing better songs all on his own. Even the middle eight of The Beatles' first great song, *Please Please Me*, is an unabashed tribute, done in the laconic Texan's unmistakable vocal style. Don Maclean was right to lament his loss in *American Pie*. It *was* the day the music died. Paul Simon lamented too. 'Where have you gone Joe

DiMaggio? A nation turns its lonely eyes to you.' What he was really asking was: Where have all the American heroes gone? Buddy Holly would have filled that void. When he died something in the American spirit died a little too. Mom's apple pie would never again be consumed with quite so much pride.

For a man who perished at the age of twenty-two, Buddy Holly left an unsurpassed musical catalogue – certainly for one at such a tender age. Can you imagine that, writing such songs at that age? *Peggy Sue, Every Day, Oh Boy!* And – of course – *That'll be the Day*, to name but a few. But there was one song of his in particular that left an indelible mark on my own life like no other.

Not his most famous song, not even his most critically-acclaimed song. It was the song my mother used to sing. When I was very young and all through my teens. The formative years. The tender years. At a time when I couldn't confront my own blossoming adolescence, let alone contemplate the skeletons in the family cupboard.

The song was *I Guess It Doesn't Matter Anymore*. A minor hit in Holly's home country and also across the Atlantic sometime around 1960, I would estimate. She would sit, when she had a quiet moment to herself, put on the record (yes, it was all vinyl back then) and sing along as Buddy Holly perkily belted out the opening lyrics. A glass of something chilled in her hand. I seem to recall white wine but it couldn't have been, for my mother never drank.

There you go and baby here am I
Well you left me here so I could sit and cry

My mother would sing along to the melody with her perfect pitch. The harmony she always heard, the harmony Buddy Holly

12

never had; McCartney's back up to Holly's orphan vocal. And then to the most incriminating piece of evidence in the next verse…

Do you remember baby last September
How you held me tight each and every night

Even as a confused sixteen year old these words gave me pause. Who exactly *was* she singing about? This song of such sweet, sad lament. It sure as hell wasn't my father. In truth, I wasn't too keen to find out. I was pretty mixed up myself, trying to deal with my parent's recent divorce. No, I wasn't too keen to delve into it at the time. But still, I wondered.

I suppose I compared Buddy Holly's own unfulfilled potential to my own, both due to circumstances out of our control – he, the circumstances of his demise, me, the circumstances of my creation. But perhaps that is drawing too long a bow. Buddy Holly's greatness and destiny for something even greater is undeniable whereas I… well perhaps I was never destined for anything extraordinary regardless of the circumstances of my creation. Certainly my sexuality was nothing to write home about. Suppressed in my teens, retarded in my twenties, there was none of Phillip Roth's Portnoy and his well-documented complaint – his adolescent riot of masturbation – from me. There was no coming in his sister's panties for this sad sack, no shooting my load into the half-pound of liver in the fridge that would shortly become the family dinner, a la Portnoy. No chasing, and bedding, all those promiscuous little shiksas. None of that for me! My adulthood followed the same course.

Mercurial at best, mediocre at worst.

Harsh words, but I won't cross them out. Soon, I will no

longer be the one in a position to judge. As I sit here in my Melbourne bedsit an old man, my time for decisive action is coming to a close. Am I an old man? I suppose by the modern measure of such things, I'm not exactly. Although I sure feel old.

It's November. The first hot, sultry day of spring. But my bedsit remains cloistered. I have yet to venture outside. The forecast says there might be a thunderstorm later on. I loved thunderstorms when I was younger, the building energy, the explosion of clouds, the flash! The crash! And then the slow release of tension. But now I am largely indifferent. Just a slight ghosting effect to those past excitements, when my future was not yet written.

Sunshine slants through the Venetian blinds, blown by a sudden gust. The sunlight splashes briefly on the vial on the mantelpiece. I eye it covetously. It's a simple vial. A clear plastic cylinder about three inches in length with a white plastic stopper, resting on its side. The clear liquid contents beckon to me. So definite. So final.

The cricket is on in the background. The first test of the season from Brisbane. It was The Ashes. Again. The Australian bowlers were terrorising the English batsmen. Again. But there is some brief respite for the English. A hailstorm has interrupted the afternoon proceedings as Australia hurtles towards victory. The camera pans over the Gabba to show the oval pockmarked with hailstones. 'The size of twenty-cent pieces,' enthuses the commentator.

Still, the weather sure beats the bleak drizzly offerings that comprise the default setting in Scotland. "Dreich" the Glaswegians call it – the perfect word. So whatever my parents did – or didn't do – I am eternally grateful for their decision to immigrate to Australia when I was just a young boy: sunshine, abundant food, opportunities. Hmm, opportunities… yes, well.

I flick open my iPhone and check the world weather. It's a little game I like to play, trying to see just how cold and miserable Glasgow is. In the background on the television, the English batsmen re-emerge onto the pitch to a combination of polite applause and jeers. Ah yes, the Glasgow forecast: Maximum 5 degrees C, cloudy. Not too bad for late autumn. Although things are set to deteriorate. Showers are forecast for the next day and later in the week, snow flurries. No peep of sun in the meteorological icons, just clouds and precipitation. But still, despite this dismal forecast I am compelled to wonder what it would be like to be transported back to that place of my birth. To the place, in truth, of which I have no recall but a disproportionate sense of curiosity. Another time, another country.

Do my advancing years make me an unreliable narrator? It is reasonable to argue "yes" but even though my body is no longer up for the chase my mind, at least, remains intact. Undoubtedly there will be those that would argue to the contrary. But cut me some slack (if I can briefly resort to the modern idiom). For what I endeavour to reveal here must, by its very nature, draw on a fair degree of speculation.

And perhaps a little faith too. For this is a reimaging of 1960s Glasgow. A reimagining of my parents and the events that led to my creation.

4

=====

PIGS IN A POKE

1960, Glasgow, Scotland...

Jude Baxter clapped her mittened hands to warm herself. Her breath came in steamy bursts. She picked up a couple of coal briquettes from the Hessian bag next to the fire and placed them on the dying embers. Then she flapped an open newspaper in front of the fire to generate an airflow. A small puff of flame obligingly ignited and began to lick at one of the coals. Satisfied, she turned to call her daughter.

'Hazel! I've got the fire going. Come out and we'll practice my lines.'

A barefoot girl in a nightgown emerged from a curtained-off section of the kitchen. She simulated the chattering of teeth.

'I'm still cold mammy. When's the fire going to warm up?'

'Just give it time. Och Hazel, for goodness sake put on your slippers. You'll catch your death.'

Jude picked up a stapled A4 script off the coffee table. *Dark at the Top of the Stairs* was printed in a neat capitalised font on the cover page. Jude flicked through to an earmarked page.

'Now,' she announced. 'I'll be Cora and you can be Sonny–'

'I don't want to be Sonny, I don't want to be a boy character,' protested the child. 'Why can't I be Lottie?'

'We're not up to there yet. You can be Lottie in the next chapter. Tell you what, read the part and I'll make you a piece and jam. Deal?'

The daughter nodded her head sceptically.

'Come closer so we can read together.'

The briquettes shifted and crackled in the grill as the coal fire gained strength.

'This is Mrs Flood in 321,' Jude began brightly, in her best Oklahoma drawl, 'I want to talk to Mr Rubin Flood at the Hotel Boomerang in Blackwell... Yes... I'll wait.'

'I'll bet he's nae there until later,' said Hazel in her best Oklahoman accent, interspersed with a little Glaswegian glottal stop at the end.

'He hasn't? Oh... I'll call back in a while then.'

Mother and daughter continued in this way for a time, with the room gradually losing its chill. Occasionally Hazel's attention would wander, brought back to focus by a reprimand from Jude.

Heavy steps could be heard on the outside landing and the door opened.

'Daddy!' said Hazel, leaping from the couch and running up to her father with an extravagant hug. She loved the smell of grease on his dungarees and sunk her face into the navy-blue depths.

'Christ, how can you read in this light? You'll go blind the pair of you.'

Jimmy turned on the light switch and then put his leather work satchel on a small table by the front door.

'Where are the boys?'

'They're still away at their pals across the landing. We'll have to go and fetch them.'

Jimmy positioned himself in front of the coal fire, facing Jude. He put his hands behind his back to warm them.

Hazel seized the opportunity to abandon her starring role as Sonny and snuck back into the kitchen alcove to play with her dollies.

'How's the play going?'

'It's hopeless,' fretted Jude. 'The first dress rehearsal is on Thursday and I've not even got half my lines memorised, and me with the lead role. I'll be the laughing stock of the Glasgow Repertory.'

'You'll be fine,' said Jimmy. 'You always are.'

He felt about in his overall pockets, took out a packet of Player's No. 6 and lit up.

'I'd like one of those too if you don't mind.'

He handed her the pack.

'What's for tea?' he asked.

'Mince 'n' tatties.'

They both took several long puffs on their cigarettes, savouring the rush of the nicotine – alone with their own thoughts.

'So, have you thought about it?'

'What's that?'

'Moving.'

Jimmy took a long, slow puff on his cigarette.

'I thought we agreed to wait six months, get sorted out financially first.'

'Och Jimmy, I don't think I can stand it any longer. And anyway we'll be fine now that I've got the part-time job at the

18

doctor's surgery.'

Jude began to tug nervously at a frayed end of the couch.

'I just don't want to bring my children up in a place like this. Look at them, sleeping three-to-a-bed in the kitchen alcove. I'd not be surprised if there's bugs in the woodwork – this place is no better than the Gorbals.'

'Hell's bloody bells, Jude! Don't exaggerate.'

Geographically they were close. And socially, perhaps, closer than they cared to admit. The other side of their street was the Plantation district, where people with aspirations were nonetheless mired in circumstances not of their making. About a kilometre beyond that was the infamous Gorbals. The residents of which did not even pretend to harbour such aspirations. And to whom violence was the answer to a good many things.

'I don't know why we can't just have peace for five minutes. Why do you always have to change everything?' said Baxter.

Jude flattened down the frayed end of the couch and said nothing.

5

=====

THE TOBACCONIST

Baxter took the shortcut up the back alley off Cathcart Road. He was out of smokes and needed to pick up a pack on the way home. He hastened along the alley – he knew the tobacconist always closed at exactly six o-clock and he only had a few minutes to spare. He spied the shop lights a few rows along in the deepening early spring twilight. The signage over the door read: *Ronald Zogalla & Sons Tobacconist*. It was funny, Baxter had patronised the store several times but had never seen these sons serving customers, or anyone else rather than Zogalla senior for that matter. Baxter had stumbled across the shop by accident – coming home from a football match involving his beloved Third Lanark – one night and had been back several times since. He found Zogalla unfailingly courteous and unhurried, two attributes not usually associated with Glaswegians.

Baxter met the proprietor at the door just as he was about to pull down the shutters. A necessity in this part of Glasgow – shopkeepers without window protection were often greeted with smashed windows on a Monday morning. Zogalla greeted Baxter by name and swung open the door of his shop. The bell over the entrance chimed merrily.

'I hope I've not come too late,' said Baxter.

'Not at all – a packet of Player's No. 6 is it?' asked Zogalla.

Without waiting for an answer, the proprietor went behind the counter and located the brand in question. Baxter put Zogalla at about five foot nine, tall for a Scot but a little under the odds for a European. One of Baxter's co-workers said the tobacconist was Swiss-Italian. He was solidly built, big-boned rather than fat, with thick, light-brown hair streaked with grey.

'Aye, that'll be fine.'

'Anything else?'

'No that'll do it. I don't want to keep you – I expect you'll want to be away home to your family for your tea,' said Baxter, his curiosity getting the better of him.

'Four shillings, please.'

Zogalla handed Baxter the pack and shot him a glance.

'There's no such rush,' said Zogalla, with just a hint of the accent of the country of his birth. 'My sons have grown up and left, they're both working in London. And you?'

'Oh, two boys and a girl. The oldest is ten. It must be hard being away from your sons.'

'They're good boys but I don't get to see them all that often. Yes it is hard sometimes,' said Zogalla, nodding his head slowly. 'They grow up so fast – would you like to see their picture?'

Baxter expected him to whip a photo out of his wallet but was instead guided to an anteroom at the back of the shop – an airless, windowless affair with a clutter of cigarette boxes and related paraphernalia. A layer of dust on several of the boxes suggested they hadn't been disturbed for quite some time.

The black-and-white portrait hung on the far wall was of a younger-looking Zogalla with two fair-haired boys and a handsome-looking woman with an intense, mischievous gaze. They were standing on a bridge over a river in the countryside.

'This photograph is taken near my hometown in Bavaria.'

'Fine looking boys,' said Baxter.

'Well, while we're back here, can I interest you in a drink? Just a quick one, I don't want to keep you from your family.'

'Aye, why not.'

Zogalla cleared the clutter from two chairs, invited Baxter to sit and produced a couple of shot glasses and a decanter of clear liquid from a nearby cupboard.

'It's schnapps,' said Zogalla, reading the quizzical look on his guest's face. 'Very popular back in my country.'

Taking elaborate care, he dispensed an even measure into both tumblers, liberal doses both. Zogalla raised his shot glass up to eye level.

'To health,' said Baxter.

'And family.'

Zogalla downed the fiery liquid in one and Baxter followed suit. It tasted crude compared to a single malt, like pure alcohol. Baxter fancied himself something of a connoisseur – Glenmorangie if you don't mind. The proprietor refilled the glasses, again taking great care, almost a reverence, with the pouring.

'Bavaria… where is that exactly?'

'In the south of Germany. Bavaria is famous for its forests, it's very beautiful.'

'Is that a fact? We don't get many Germans in Glasgow.'

'I'm not surprised,' said Zogalla. 'It hasn't always been fun, I can tell you. Especially during the war… especially with young children.'

Zogalla gave a low laugh, which Baxter found impossible to decipher.

'What did you do during the war Mister Baxter?'

'Please, it's Jimmy.'

'What did you do during the war, Jimmy? Did you fight?'

'Well no. I was stationed in Glasgow actually, at the Hillington Aircraft Factory.'

'I know of it.'

Baxter cleared his throat. 'I was helping to build the gears for the Rolls-Royce Merlin engines that went into the British Bombers. I'm an engineer by trade, you see.'

'What sort of aircraft?'

'Spitfires and the like.'

It occurred to Baxter that he had put engines in planes that bombed his host's country; German cities, with German people in them. The pair endured an uncomfortable silence while they assessed how they felt to be in the company of someone of a nationality who, until very recently, had been their greatest adversary. But the two men took a sip of their drinks and the awkward moment passed. Baxter couldn't imagine what sort of circumstances had led this man to Scotland but felt he had pried enough for one day.

'Please,' said Zogalla, 'have a cigarette. Nothing tastes better after a schnapps.'

Baxter took one from the pack and offered one to his host, who waved it away.

'I'm trying to give up. Something that takes willpower – something I seem to have less and less these days. Or maybe I'm just getting old.'

Baxter lit up and puffed away contentedly, while the

proprietor looked on enviously.

'You know,' said Zogalla, 'I don't why I told you I was German. I'm usually more cautious.'

Baxter waved the comment away.

'I've gotten by telling people here I'm Italian. I can get away with it because of my surname. Things are a lot better now. Feelings have cooled off, you might say. But all the same, I'd appreciate it if you keep it to yourself.'

'No bother,' said the Scot.

'Well, how about one more for the road?' said Zogalla.

'That'd be grand.'

As the proprietor poured, Baxter examined the family portrait on the wall again. And the eyes of the striking woman.

'Where's your wife?' he asked suddenly.

There was a pause.

'She died several years ago. Lung cancer.'

'I'm so sorry to hear that.'

'Now you know,' said the German, as he stoppered the decanter, 'why I'm so determined to give up smoking.'

6

=====

THE WEDDING

Jimmy and Jude Baxter were invited to the wedding of one of
Jimmy's colleagues from the tool shop. Baxter always found such
social gatherings a chore, getting done up in a suit and tie like a
pox doctor's clerk. He'd owned the outfit for ten years and it was
still too tight around the chest. He had meant to get it altered but
somehow never got round to it. Then there was the business of
cleaning the grime from under his fingernails after a week cutting
gears. He'd rather be away in the stands at Cathkin watching
Third Lanark, but it was a mate's wedding, so what could you
do. Jude, on the other hand, loved nothing better than to get done
up for a social gathering and shine. *'Just like she does in the theatre,'*
thought Baxter. She claimed to be insecure in front of new people
– but she always seemed to lap up the attention.

The pair were waiting in the lobby of the function room. The
wedding vows were complete and the ensemble was awaiting the
triumphant arrival of the bride and groom. Free drinks and
nibbles were on offer – appreciated and indulged in to the full by
the grateful Glaswegian throng, who did not need to be asked
twice.

Jimmy and Jude were off to the side, admiring one of the

paintings that adorned the walls.

'Yes I thought I might find you two here – quite an impressive collection isn't it?'

The best man had joined them and with him was a fair, tallish man with a slightly receding hairline.

'Colin McAllister, I'd like you to meet Jimmy Baxter and his lovely wife Jude.'

The two men shook hands.

'Colin's an old school chum,' said the best man. 'But you could say he's made good since then – he's put us all to shame.'

'Nonsense,' said Colin. 'I've just had a spot of luck or two.'

'You two have a lot in common,' added the best man. 'Jimmy's quite the art-lover.'

'Aye well, Jude's the artistic one, what with all her singing and interest in the theatre. I just plonk away on the guitar occasionally.'

'That's quite a piece of work,' observed Colin, as the best man left them to get acquainted.

Briefly, the three admired the painting in silence. It was of a beautiful young Chinese woman seated in a white cheongsam dress looking directly at the viewer, a Mona Lisa smile ghosting across her face. She held a tiny red shoe in one hand and a length of silk thread in the other, the thread was held in her pursed lips so she could gain purchase as she sewed it into the shoe. She was surrounded by a number of decorative vases.

'That looks like one of those terrible wee shoes they make women wear in China,' said Jude.

'I think the practice is dying out,' said Colin.

'Thank goodness for that.'

The stranger moved closer to the painting.

'This is good, extremely good. Hmm... an original too, although it's unsigned. Look at those brushstrokes, you don't usually see this style in Britain. The venue owner must have picked it up from the Far East. I'd say it'd fetch quite a price at auction. I wonder if he knows exactly how much it's worth. I'll have to have a word with him later.'

'You're very knowledgeable,' said Baxter.

'Occupational hazard, you might say.'

Colin fished in his wallet and handed Baxter a business card, identifying him as the director of Prestige Art.

'I'm an art dealer and an auctioneer, so it's in my interest to know the worth of things. You should pop by the gallery sometime – we've a number of fine works.'

'Aye, I will. That sounds grand.'

There was a stirring at the entrance.

'I'd better go and say hello,' said Jimmy. 'Some of my colleagues have just arrived. I'll leave Jude to entertain you. Excuse me.'

Colin favoured him with a quick smile as he walked away.

Jude continued to stare intently at the painting, suddenly uncomfortable in the presence of this over-confident man – slightly taller and so much better dressed than her husband. What her mother would refer to as a "fancy man".

'You know,' said Colin, 'I thought this was going to be a real dull affair. No-one told me that there would be anyone as lovely as you here.'

Jude took him in with a sidelong glance. She felt the colour rising a little in her cheeks.

'You look like royalty in that get-up, a princess,' said Colin, admiring her purple dress.

She couldn't help but laugh a little at the absurdity of it. It was, in fact, one of her favourites, which she had chosen to wear for the event after a great deal of deliberation, much to her husband's frustration.

'All the vases have wee faces in them,' observed Jude. 'It's so surreal. Look at the one on the right, it looks like a fat man in a tuxedo – or am I imagining it?'

'That's a sign of great art, the more you look the more you see. It wouldn't surprise me if this was one of the Asian masters.'

'You *do* know a lot about art.'

'Well, they didn't think much of me at the Glasgow School of Art,' he said with a deprecating laugh. 'Sadly, they were right. I realised that I didn't have "the gift", as they say. But I discovered something else, I have an eye for identifying a piece of art, and putting a price to it. That's what I'm *very* good at.'

A waiter came by with a tray-full of flutes of champagne. With one smooth action, Colin scooped up two glasses from the tray.

'Would you care for one?' he enquired.

'Well, I'd rather not – I don't usually drink.'

'Oh come on,' he cajoled, pressing a glass into her palm. 'Just the one.'

She turned to face him as she accepted the glass, becoming a little flustered by the light touch of fingers.

'How about yourself – do you enjoy the arts?' Colin asked.

'I don't know much about it, I'm afraid. But I do appreciate good literature. I'm quite the bookworm. Do you read yourself?'

'When I can find the time. What are you reading now?'

'*Lady Chatterley's Lover.*'

Colin let out a low whistle.

'By D. H. Lawrence.'

'I know who wrote it. That book was banned, you know.'

'But not anymore. The world is opening up. People are becoming more adventurous.'

Jude was feeling light-headed. Drinking was a rarity for her. So why was she sipping champagne with a man she didn't much like? And probably a scoundrel into the bargain – but at least he was a handsome one. With those composed grey eyes and his irritating ghost of a grin – so cock-sure of himself.

'Lovely, lovely Jude.'

Her eyes met his.

'Isn't there a Saint Jude?' he said, holding her gaze.

'Patron saint of lost causes,' she replied. 'Sometimes I think my marriage is a lost cause.'

She laughed to let him know she was making a joke.

A bell rang out to signal to the ensemble to take their seats.

'Oh great, the speeches,' said Colin, with mock enthusiasm. 'Well, it was a pleasure,' he said, taking her fingers with one of those dainty male-female handshakes. 'I hope to bump into you again soon.'

'Glasgow is quite small, isn't it?'

7

=====

SNOW

I lied. I do have one memory of Scotland. Actually I'm not even sure if it's a memory at all, perhaps just a memory of a memory, like a grainy, black-and-white movie reel in my head – so I'm not sure it counts. I would have been about two years old at the time. I must have left our tenement building and I was outside playing. Probably lured out by the thick layer of snow covering the ground. I looked around but all I could see were tenement buildings in every direction. The same identical grey brick walls, each with an identical close. I couldn't identify which close was ours. There wasn't one soul around. I was alone and lost!

Even though the street was covered in snow, it must have been near freezing or below but I had no recollection of cold (does a young child ever recall or even *feel* cold?). Only fear. I screamed out for someone. No one came. I began bawling. It seemed like an eternity but it must have only been moments, a minute at most. My mother appeared at the mouth of one of the closes. She had come to rescue me. She cooed and called me home. Was my mother smiling? This is just a memory of a memory after all, but the way I figure it, she must have been.

Alasdair Gray (a writer of magic realism fiction) describes memory as:

An editing process that inevitably exaggerates some episodes, suppresses others and arranges events in neater orders.

I hold this to be true. But I swear my memory of being lost in the snow – however briefly – happened exactly as I have described it here. Perhaps that's the way of it with the early memories, the big memories. The great moments in our lives. Or perhaps these are the most corrupted of all.

In any event, my episode of being lost in the snow was a long time ago. When my life was a blank canvas. Before I threw in my lot with crooks and swindlers, zigged when I should have zagged, tossed the coin and called wrongly – and lived to rue the consequences. Watching on from the wings as others prospered from my foolishness.

The weather has turned. It's been hot all week but a cool change has swept in overnight, a southerly buster, sending in bursts of wind and cloud and rain punctuated by blue sky and sunshine. But the atmosphere in my bedsit remains largely unchanged. I haven't ventured outside yet. But that's not surprising; I often don't make it out even on a good day.

It's only mid-December but Australia is already leading England three-nil in the cricket. The Ashes have been won back before Christmas. The Boxing Day Test is going to be an anticlimax now. But people will still go along to the Melbourne Cricket Ground to watch. Or follow the game on their car radio as they drive down to the coast on their summer holidays. Or on a television dragged out to the patio at Boxing Day barbeques, and occasionally watched while people chomp on their sausages

31

and salad and drink and chat. Pretending it still matters, pretending to have a good time, in that way people do.

The room suddenly darkens as a swift-moving cloud blots out the sun. The vial is still on the mantelpiece. Upright this time. The liquid in repose. I don't remember moving it but sometimes I pick it up and finger it unconsciously – greedily – like Gollum with his "precious" in *Lord of the Rings*. But why wouldn't I treasure it? It offers me a chance at the most valuable gift of all (at least at this stage of proceedings) and I want to keep it safe. Its time will come sooner than you know.

8

=====

THE BOMBING OF DRESDEN

'I would like to apologise on behalf of my countrymen for the Clydebank Blitz. All those lives lost, homes destroyed – the Scottish people did not deserve it.'

Baxter had made a habit of popping in on the tobacconist on the way home from work whenever he needed cigarettes. And sometimes when he didn't, he was surprised how much he enjoyed the company of this middle-aged German, sitting in the back of his tobacco shop chatting about matters large and small. Baxter had a growing admiration for the tobacconist – a man who had kept his dignity and sense of perspective despite having lost so much. Their talks had been far ranging but the one subject the pair had not broached had been the war. Baxter was taken aback by the sudden confession.

Baxter remembered the Clydebank Bombing vividly. It had taken place over two apocalyptic nights. It had seemed the whole of Glasgow was being blown to smithereens. The German bombers were targeting Glasgow's shipyard on the Clyde River in a pre-emptive strike in an attempt to weaken the British naval force. As a young man called into service of the Royal Air Force, he was acquainted with many people who worked on the Clyde and had known people who had perished during the attacks.

'Terrible things happen during wartime,' said Baxter. 'There's no need to apologise.'

To show there were no hard feelings, Baxter lit up a Player's No. 6 and offered one to the German, who declined.

'I must say,' observed Baxter, 'you're the first person I've seen who runs a tobacco shop that doesn't smoke.'

'The world is full of paradoxes. Actually, I think I will have something. Somehow today, I think I need a lift.'

Zogalla leaned forward in his chair and pulled out a box of cigars from a nearby cupboard.

'But on the rare occasions I smoke these days, I prefer these. Would you care for one?'

'A little rich for my blood,' said the Scot.

Zogalla plucked a cigar from the box, held a match to the end and puffed on it profusely, becoming surrounded in small billows of smoke, like Chief Sitting Bull at a powwow, Baxter thought. The sweet, delicious aroma filled the room. Baxter loved the smell but the one time he had actually smoked a cigar it had been a disappointment. It was simply overpowering.

'If I may be so bold Ronald,' ventured the Scot, 'I'm curious to know what it was that made you leave your homeland. You seem to look back on your life in Germany with a certain degree of fondness.'

Zogalla stared reflectively at the burning ember of his cigar.

'There was a time in Germany when people of an artistic temperament were not very popular. Also journalists.'

'Which were you?'

'Both.'

The German laughed bitterly.

34

'Yes, Mister Hitler and his friends didn't approve of people like me. "Subversives" he called us. What a joke.'

'So when did you leave Germany?'

'Leave? It was more like forced – we had no choice. 1935.'

'So, you would have been here when Glasgow was bombed.'

'Yes I was here for that. Can you imagine, being bombed by your own people? But I missed the bombings in Germany, which were far worse.'

'I'm not so sure about that.'

Baxter refrained from mentioning The Holocaust, which seemed to crowd the room like a very cumbersome elephant.

'I can understand your position,' said the tobacconist. 'But the victors write their own version of history, the British press had its own rose-coloured view. Are you familiar, by any chance, with the Bombing of Dresden?'

'Of course.'

Baxter knew of it, knew there had been a significant death toll. But in truth, since the war had ended he had thought very little about it or anything else connected with it. He had heard rumours that something truly horrible had happened but then a lot of crazy rumours circulated after the war ended. Mostly unsubstantiated. Like most people in Glasgow, he thought it best to forget about the great conflict and get on with his own life. He had a wife and kids to feed, football matches to attend, boxing matches to win. Life went on.

'Do you know,' continued Zogalla quietly, 'How many people died during the air raid on Dresden?'

'I know it was a lot.'

'Over 400,000.'

'I can see you're sceptical. Let me show you something.'

35

Zogalla pulled a well-thumbed book from a nearby drawer. It was in German, although judging from the lurid shot of artillery fire on the cover, it was war related. The tobacconist flicked through the book.

'Here,' the German flipped the book around and slid it along the table to Baxter.

'I doubt you can't speak German but the pictures, I believe, paint a thousand words – or in this case, four-hundred thousand.'

Baxter studied the grainy black-and-white images. Each one depicted a scene of utter desolation, of fire-scorched earth and the skeletal wreckage of houses. One picture, with an entire page dedicated to it, caught his attention. It was taken from the point of view of a large stone sculpture of a robed man looking down on the devastation, a hand outstretched as if imploring the viewer to take in the entirety of the scene. Below, and as far as the eye can see are the outer structure of buildings – like catacombs – strewn over a pock-marked moonscape. There was a caption below the photograph. Baxter could make no sense of it, except for the figure 400,000–450,000.

'The death toll from the Bombing of Dresden as officially released by British Intelligence was 25,000. Now take a look at this picture and tell me how this can be so.'

'I have never seen images such as these before. The… scale of this is much worse than anything I imagined.'
Baxter could not take his eyes off the statue looking down on the utter desolation of the obliterated city.

'Dresden was a city of 750,00 people' Zogalla put a finger to the image, it was quivering slightly. 'Now tell me how it is possible that only 25,000 died.'

To Baxter's eye it looked like no-one could have survived at all.

'Dresden was bombed so heavily that a firestorm was created. That engulfed the city and everyone in its path. People died in their bunkers from lack of oxygen. Look at this statue, such a symbol of peace. Do you know what this statue is called? In German it is *Die Gute*, which means "The Good". God seems to have quite a sense of irony, eh? Having The Good look down on such an evil act?'

Baxter looked into the face of the German, which had an ashen look. He looked unwell.

'I'm shocked by this, I never knew. It's truly awful,' Baxter finally managed. He put a hand on the German's shoulder.

'Dresden was a city of art and culture. Of churches and wonderful architecture,' Zogalla said quietly. 'It was not directly involved in the war, Germany was about to surrender. So why was it bombed? I have read a lot about this but no-one has a definite answer.'

'I'm surprised Germany didn't make more of a fuss about it.'

'The country was humiliated by the defeat in the war. The German people are a proud people, perhaps to have its citizens slaughtered on such a scale was a source of shame. And maybe, just maybe, there was guilt over what the Nazis did, over their own terrible acts.'

Zogalla suddenly clapped his hands together.

'Ah, let's not dwell on all this unpleasantness. I shouldn't have brought it up. Let's have some Schnapps and forget about it.' The German became busy, making a show of bringing out the glasses and the decanter. He even started to hum a little tune. But Baxter's eyes remained fixed on the statue, looking down on the ruined city.

9

=====

A GAME OF SNOOKER

Baxter began to ride to and from work on a newly acquired pushbike. The streets were often treacherous. What with icy roads in winter, slick, wet roads in spring and impatient lorry drivers hurtling past on the busy Cathcart Road at any time of year threatening to sideswipe him. But it was too far to walk and he couldn't afford a car so what could you do.

He arrived home to an empty flat. There was a note from Jude telling him there was a plate of stovies in the oven for his tea and that she had taken the kids to visit their granny. The fire had died down and there was a decided chill in the air. He added a few briquettes and stoked it up. He lit a cigarette and made himself a cup of tea. It was a rare treat to have the place to himself. The children were usually running amok with their pals or Jude busy housecleaning, singing at the top of her lungs as she went – typically a Frank Sinatra number.

As the kettle began to whistle Baxter began to contemplate. Following Zogalla's revelation about Dresden, he found himself compelled to take stock of his role in the war. And reassess the consequences. On some vague level, of course, he was aware that he had built engines that were put in British bombers that then dropped the bombs in foreign countries. He had even experienced a measure of guilt that he was not fighting on the front line against the enemy like so many of his pals but rather remaining back in Glasgow, like some sort of coward. But he was assured by those around that his work at Hillington – sanctioned by the Air Ministry to make bombers for the RAF – was important work. That his skill as an engineer was helping to protect Britain during the war effort. That he was playing his part.

But he had not been forced to confront the stark reality of his involvement until Zogalla had shown him the pictures of Dresden. That, in all likelihood, he had put engines in planes that had killed people. Lots of people. The images of a firebombed Dresden haunted him. But surely Zogalla's death toll was fanciful. Four hundred thousand killed? Surely not. Surely just the inflated ramblings of embittered German war scholars. But nevertheless, it gave him a determination to make good. What was done could not be undone but decided, well, if not to redeem himself exactly because he had only been playing his part in the war, then at least to make amends a little.

But, as always, life pressed. And the demands of three young children and a theatrical wife crowded out other concerns. Jude was making her debut in the lead role of *Dark at the Top of the Stairs* with the Glasgow Repertory later that week. Baxter usually tried to avoid the palaver of attending Jude's various acting roles with the repertory group – especially opening night – but this time would be different. His thoughts turned to Colin McAllister. He had recently been to visit his gallery and the art dealer had been most cordial, even offering to secure Baxter a couple of hard-to-come-by tickets (it was officially sold out) for an upcoming Scottish FA Cup fixture at Hampden. Colin was a self-confessed lover of the local art scene, and more than once had boasted about his connections to Glasgow actors and casting companies, Baxter decided to invite Colin along to the opening night. Plus, he had an ulterior motive for the call. Maybe Colin could use his connections to help Jude break into the big time.

Time for decisive action. Baxter stubbed out his cigarette and phoned the art dealer, catching him just as he was about to leave the gallery. They bantered about the football for a while and Third Lanark's remarkable season so far – sitting just by Celtic and Rangers on the league table – and then Baxter came to the point.

'Do you play snooker, by any chance?'

'I haven't played since art school,' said Colin, 'But I was quite keen at one stage.'

'We could have a friendly game or two at my local snooker hall. The tables are reasonable. Or at least level. My shout – I'd like to pay you back for the football tickets.'

'Why not,' said Colin, warming to the idea. 'Don't expect me to play like Walter Donaldson, but at least I can hold the right end of the cue.'

The two men met at Baxter's snooker hall the following Monday. It was a smoky, dimly-lit, all-male affair with rows of snooker tables. The green felt of each table was lit up by a pair of naked light bulbs. The light from each table was obscured by small tasselled curtains that circled above each table's perimeter. The snooker hall had a no-alcohol policy. But as long as patrons were surreptitious about it and didn't cause trouble, the owners turned a blind eye. Players could often be seen having a 'wee dram' from a bottle of something hidden in a brown paper bag mid-game. But Baxter had no intention of drinking on this night, he wanted to keep a clear head.

He lost the coin toss and Colin asked him to break. Rather than take the safe option and clip the last red from the triangle of fifteen balls like most players, Baxter recklessly smashed the white ball into the pack scattering reds in all directions, as was his habit. As luck would have it one of the reds bounced off several cushions, rolled up to a side pocket and dropped gently in. Baxter potted a black and another red in quick succession. The white ball angled across the table to give a very gettable shot on the blue. Baxter's game, it seemed, was on. Although the fact that he was playing stone-cold sober for once probably helped.

'You play well,' said Colin.

'Aye, well it's a sure sign of a wasted youth.'

Baxter decided to fluff the shot on the blue. It wouldn't do to embarrass his opponent with a thrashing, especially one he was going to ask a favour of.

'Hard lines,' said Colin, as the blue ball jammed in the jaws of the corner pocket and stayed out.

As Colin lined up his shot, Baxter walked over to the scoreboard – a sort of horizontal abacus – and tallied up his break of nine.

'Are you related to the Pollokshaws Baxters by any chance?' asked Colin

'No, I don't know of them. In fact I don't know any Baxters in Glasgow at all. Well, the thing is you see, I never knew my father.'

Colin looked at Baxter with an appraising eye.

'Must've been tough growing up in Glasgow with that hanging over you are head.'

Colin chalked his cue stick with a professional air and then hovered over the white ball in a study of concentration, but unfortunately miscued, drawing a foul and giving away four points. Baxter dutifully slid the peg on his scoreboard across four notches.

'I won't lie to you,' said Baxter. 'It was at times. You feel cheated in some ways, like something's missing inside.'

Baxter rarely opened up about this sensitive topic, least of all to a man he hardly knew. But something about Colin's gentlemanly demeanour seemed to invite the sharing of a confidence.

'I guess that's why I don't feel comfortable with women. Don't get me wrong I adore them, it's just that I don't find them easy to talk to you.'

'Well you've done wonderfully well with Jude,' said Colin, matter of factly.

A solitary moth began to flutter crazily around one of the naked light bulbs over their table.

'I'm glad you mentioned her,' said Baxter, 'There's something I'd like to invite you along to.'

Baxter thumped the cue ball into a red which went unerringly into the dead centre of a corner pocket with a thud. It seemed he could do no wrong.

'I remember you saying that you're quite passionate about the local theatre scene,' he continued. 'Trying to promote fresh talent and all.'

'Definitely,' said Colin.

'Would you like to come along and see the opening night of Jude's new play? Look, I know Glasgow Repertory is only wee, not like the grand productions you're used to attending. But they're a good crowd. And the plays they put on are surprisingly entertaining.'

The black ball was hovering over a side pocket. It would look too suspicious to miss such an easy shot, so Baxter casually potted it.

'You don't need to convince me,' laughed Colin, 'I'm keen to come along. What's the production?'

'Eh? Oh, *Dark at the Top of the Stairs*.'

'I'm vaguely familiar with it.'

'It's set in Oklahoma,' said Baxter, warming to his task. 'All the actors put on these fantastic accents from the deep south. Wait until you see Jude perform – you wouldn't recognise her.'

'I can hardly wait.'

At the end of the frame, Colin had potted a grand total of six balls. Four reds, a yellow and a pink. Baxter had gifted him two fouls, bringing Colin's score to the princely sum of twenty. Despite his worst efforts, Baxter won the frame handsomely with a score of sixty-two.

'How about another frame?' said Colin. 'I think I've dusted off the cobwebs.'

10

=====

OPENING NIGHT

The two men met in the foyer shortly before the curtain call. Part of a babbling throng of the cognoscenti and cognoscenti wannabes. Jude briefly appeared from backstage – a bundle of heightened senses as the opening approached, revelling in her distress.

'Jude, do you remember Colin from the wedding?' said Baxter. 'He's quite an admirer of the local acting scene.'

'Jimmy's told me all about your impressive body of work.' Not realising he had been invited, she took in Colin with a look of wide-eyed surprise.

'It's an honour to have you here,' she finally managed. Jude looked around with a mix of dread and anticipation at the crowd still spilling through the repertory doors. She bid her new admirer a quick goodbye and headed backstage for her costume change.

The theatre-goers were ushered through to their seats by a bell ringer dressed somewhat in the style of Jean Lafitte, all sweeping coattails and a pirate's hat adorned by a couple of flapping ostrich feathers – quite the spectacle as he circled the foyer and clanged his bell with a flourish.

The theatre was about three-quarters full – a good turnout for an amateur repertory group opening night. As the lights dimmed and the crumpled crimson curtain began to rise on squeaky castors, the crowd became hushed in expectation. After that, it seemed to Baxter, came something of an anticlimax. As these productions invariably were. It just looked like a bunch of people under bright lights dressed up in silly costumes, putting on silly voices, surrounded by silly props – like children who never grew up. Baxter was baffled by their need to do this. Still, after a while he got swept up in the story. It was about a frightened and insecure boy pining for his absent father – something that Baxter could keenly relate to.

It always gave him a start when he recognised Jude, away from her role as a tenements housewife. A ravishing stranger – this one in a farmer's peasant dress – with a strange new personality that made him think there was a lot more to her than he would ever know. Colin seemed quite absorbed in the whole thing, maintaining rapt attention throughout. Occasionally he leant towards Baxter to whisper praise for some detail of Jude's performance.

As the play drew to a close it seemed, to Baxter's untrained eye that the performance had gone well, without any obvious stuff-ups or too egregious fluffing of lines. Jude's performance, he felt, had been flawless.

'*Now Sonny*,' she drawled, her voice confidently projecting across the theatre. '*It's time for your bed young man.*'

'*But Mom, it's dark at the top of the stairs.*'

'*Don't you worry none, there's nothing to be scared of. Daddy will be home soon.*'

The boy actor began doggedly climbing the prop stairs.

Finally, the curtain comes down and there was a ripple of applause which quickly escalated to an avalanche. And when the curtain came up and the actors all bowed in unison, the audience renewed its cheering. Colin rose to his feet and clapped and shouted 'Bravo!' as vigorously as any in the theatre. Baxter was pleased.

11

=====

A DRUBBING

Baxter turned the corner and saw a knot of men with their backs to him. They were kicking out at someone on the ground. He recognised the coat of the victim. Zogalla! He watched the scene unfold in slow motion, as if in a dream. He saw the tobacconist try to stand, only to be kicked back down again.

'Oi! Get the fuck away!' he shouted.

With the same unreal sense, Baxter ran up to the men, scattering them as he pushed through between the attackers and their victim. Now all eyes were on him as he turned to face them. He had the conch, as his mother used to say. The men all wore heavy coats and woollen royal blue scarves.

'*Oh fuck, Rangers supporters,*' thought Baxter, with an odd sense of calm. '*This isn't going to end well.*' Celtic had handed Rangers a three-nil drubbing that afternoon at Parkhead. He could smell alcohol on their collective breath, no doubt a combination of Tenants Lager and cheap whisky. So they were pissed up and pissed off.

'Stay out of things that don't concern you, James Baxter.'

He flinched at the formal mention of his name.

The owner of the voice was away to his right. His face was

partially obscured by a Rangers beanie but he recognised the man as a former workmate – he had been sacked for constantly turning up to work drunk. He was also a sidekick of feared gang leader Wee Alec. But he hadn't seen either man since their boxing proposition at Glasgow Gym.

'This man's a mate of mine,' said Baxter. 'Leave him alone Willie – he's done no harm.'

Baxter was aware that behind him Zogalla had not moved, but he dared not turn his back to take a look. He felt a small surge of relief that Wee Alec was not among the gang of hooligans. With a bit of luck he might be able to stare this lot down.

'No harm? We found him reading this.'

Baxter's ex-workmate picked up a sheet of crumpled newspaper off the street and shoved it towards his face.

'It's a newspaper, a German newspaper. *Der Spiegel. Der fucking Spiegel.* This man's a fucking Nazi. He didn't much like it when we rubbed his face in this filth, I can tell you.'

A few of the men tittered.

'Leave him be,' said Baxter.

'And he's a Catholic into the bargain,' chimed in someone else.

One of the assailants had spied a silver crucifix cross around Zogalla's neck. It had been ripped from his body and flung onto the roof of a nearby tenement.

'What are you trying to be James Baxter, some sort of Good Samaritan? Don't forget, no good deed goes unpunished,' he threatened. 'I thought you'd know that growing up on the streets. Don't interfere.'

'This man just runs a tobacco shop. He's harmless,' said Baxter.

'Is that a fact?' said a short, squat man pushing through the throng towards Baxter, apparently the ringleader.

'See you,' he said, his eyes pinpricks of fury, 'fuck off!'
Baxter kept his ground. The man lunged at Baxter with a wild
uppercut. He evaded the punch and sent the man sprawling with
a neat right jab. Another came at him from the left but before he
could get a punch in, he was clobbered in the side of the head
with a bottle from the right. His legs gave way and he staggered
onto his hands and knees just as the ringleader got to his feet.

'Right, I'm going to do you cunt.'

The ringleader swung a right boot into Baxter's guts, knocking
the wind out of him and sending him face down onto the
pavement. Instinct took over and he covered his head with his
arms. As every Glasgow street fighter knows, when it all goes
tits-up you have to keep your head covered at all costs. Then it all
went black.

When Baxter came too, the first thing he noticed was Zogalla's
motionless body. Then the shrill ringing in his ears. It dawned on
him that it was the sound of a whistle. A blue blur went past him.
He tried to sit up. He was instantly greeted by a shooting pain in
his ribs. He put his hand to his jaw, which he moved
experimentally from side to side. Everything seemed to be intact
but he had a fat lip and the taste of blood in his mouth. Someone
must have got a boot or a fist in while he was unconscious. And
he had a monstrous lump on the side of his head and the mother
of all headaches. Then the world seemed to be spinning.

'Hey Charlie, forget it. I've got one here.'

The blue blur slowed and stopped. A copper. Baxter was
hauled to his feet, cuffed and frogmarched unceremoniously to
Govan Police Station.

12

=====

CAKE

Jude was alone with her mother in her flat on Cartside Street. As always, it was overheated and stuffy. She could never recall her mother ever opening a window. Aside from the ponderous clunking of the grandfather clock next to the mantlepiece, the only sound was the occasional thud of a football. Jude had taken the children to see their gran but after a perfunctory 'hello granny', the boys had wasted no time bolting downstairs for a kick. Hazel had, of course, trailed after them like an obedient dog.

Her mother emerged from the kitchen with a tray and began fussing over the pouring of the tea. Jude was still basking in the warm glow of the opening of *Dark at the Top Stairs*. The presence of the handsome stranger – Jimmy's pal Colin – had added a little frisson to the triumph of the night. Silly she knew but the buzz was undeniable. Nevertheless, a familiar knot of tension formed in her stomach as she watched her mother pour.

Jude's mother had a thick head of hair gone completely white, and favoured a long, woolly turquoise-coloured cardigan. She had a peaceful face, graced with grandmotherly lines that to the impartial eye looked kindly.

The Swiss roll, evenly sliced, was on a plate next to the cups. It was one of her mother's favourites – homemade by spreading strawberry jam over a layer of sponge cake and rolling it into a cylinder. She could remember her mother making it in the kitchen from a very young age. But it was not a source of fondness. It seemed to Jude, that when she visited her mother with her sisters she always got the smallest piece of Swiss roll. But on this occasion it was just her and her mammy, so she had nothing to compare the size of the slice to. At least she was *getting* a slice. Still, she remembered. As a child, Jude was never allowed any of the Swiss roll at all. She picked up a piece from the plate and took a bite and began to chew. She looked at her mother and even though no words were exchanged, she still managed to make Jude feel guilty, even for this small indulgence, as she watched her daughter eat.

From the apartment window, Jude could see the children kicking the football around on a grassy strip next to the River Cart. A surprising splash of green in the overwhelming grey of Glasgow's tenements.

She opened the window and called out to them, 'Come up and get some cake.'

'In a minute,' called back Gregor.

They were playing a game of keepings off and Hazel was in the middle, the boys easily dribbling past her and passing the ball to each other.

'And don't make Hazel go in the middle all the time', added Jude.

'But mammy, she always loses the ball,' complained Billy.

'Don't go too near the water,' she said as a parting shot, before closing the window. The river, a tributary of the Clyde, was presently shallow and slow-moving, no wider than a canal. But it was prone to flash flooding from sustained downpours – leading to sodden misery for the residents of Cartside, and neighbouring, streets.

'Honestly Jude,' said her mother. 'You've got such lovely boys. I don't know why you waste all your time with that acting nonsense. You should be home looking after your weans.'

It pained Jude that her mother had never been to a single night of one of her plays. She had hoped so desperately that she would come but her mother scoffed at her daughter's acting aspirations. Jude had long since given up asking her to attend.

'Och it does no harm, I spend plenty of time with the children,' said Jude.

'But you could be with them more, especially with Jimmy out all hours playing snooker and the like.'

'You know he comes home late because he's working overtime,' snapped Jude, taking her mother's bait. 'He doesn't go out with his pals all that often. But when he does he deserves it – he works hard.'

Nit-picking over her husband's shortcomings, it seemed to Jude, was one of her mother's pet subjects. The fact that he had never known his father was another – as if it was somehow his fault, a flaw in his character. Jude always felt compelled to defend him.

'And I don't know why you've started that job in the doctor's surgery,' continued her mother. 'Can he not even make enough money to support his own family?'

'That's not it at all,' said Jude. 'We have no problem making ends meet.'

'I suppose you want to move, is that it? Govan not good enough for you. Eadies have been living in Govan for generations and it's always been good enough for us.'

Jude took a deep breath and said nothing. Her mother knew perfectly well Govan had been built less than fifty years ago, no time for the Eadies or anyone else to have 'lived there for generations'. It was just another of her mother's silly little ways of taunting her.

The children piled into the flat, breathing hard from their dash up the stairs.

'Oh here you are,' said their grandmother, with genuine warmth in her voice. 'Come and have some cake.'

It never ceased to amaze Jude how gentle her mother was with her grandchildren, now revelling in their small stampede towards the food. She seemed to soften in their presence. Jude found it touching but hurtful too, underscoring, as it did, her own distant relationship with her mother.

'Make sure you don't spill any crumbs on the carpet,' said Jude, as each of her children took a slice of Swiss roll from their grandmother and began to devour the treat with gusto.

There had only ever been one occasion in her life that Jude could recall her mother adopting a softer tone with her. It was the first time she had held Gregor, in the very room they were in now. The first-born Baxter could have been no more than two weeks old.

'Oh he's so beautiful,' her mother said in a tender voice, as she cradled the infant in her arms.

'Was I awful hard on you when you were young?' her mother had asked in a voice Jude barely recognised. 'I didn't mean to be you know. It's just times were so hard when you were small.'

It was the closest she ever got to an apology from her mother for her treatment as a child. The only bright spot Jude remembered from a bond of maternal knife twisting. A torment that had given her a lifelong ambition to escape her own skin.

13

=====

THE POLIS

Baxter suffered the indignity of being held, handcuffed, in a receiving cell while he waited to be interviewed. As it was still relatively early on a Saturday the cell was not crowded, just Baxter and one other – an old man, presumably hauled in for drunk and disorderly. He wore a tattered beige coat that stank of piss and spent most of the time slumped on a bench along the wall. He interspersed with asking Baxter for 'a wee ciggie' this with a sporadic – slurred but surprisingly loud in the echoey chamber – rendition of *I Belong to Glasgow*. The coppers outside occasionally told him to pipe down. All the while, Baxter sat quietly on the opposite bench. His head began to throb mightily and he worried about the condition of Zogalla. He had asked the coppers while being led up to the police station but they remained tight-lipped. After an unpleasant hour with the would-be baritone, Baxter was led to another room and told to sit.

'You can take the cuffs off this one, he doesn't look like a killer,' said a man on the opposite side of the desk. The constables did as they were bid and left. The man held Baxter in a penetrating gaze for a time, as if he had seen it all before, before turning his eyes in an unhurried fashion to the incident report on his desk.

He reminded Baxter of the policeman in the *Oor Wullie* comic strip, who was always chasing Wullie and his pals for some high-spirited mischief. He had the same pronounced jaw line and beady eyes. Although this policeman had neatly trimmed coppery-red hair (crowning a bald pate) and a toothbrush moustache to match. A mug of coffee was before him on the desk. Baxter thought he detected a whiff of alcohol rising with the vapour. The officer kept his eyes down over the document for about a minute. Finally satisfied, he took a sip from his coffee cup, plucked a pen from his desk, flipped over the page and looked up.

'Name?'

'Jim-James Baxter.'

'Do you not know your own name?'

'James Baxter.'

'Age?'

'Thirty-eight.'

'Address?'

'Twenty-nine Govanhill Street.'

'There you go, you're getting the hang of it. Occupation?'

'Engineer.'

'Place of employment?'

'Crockatt's.'

Baxter watched the police officer through the prism of his aching head, while he made entries in his notebook. Baxter wanted to ask for an Aspirin but didn't want to give the police officer the satisfaction of saying no. So he focused on the name placard on the desk instead, which read SUPT Alastair Middlemiss – seemingly too short to display the unabbreviated version of his title.

'I don't know why you're keeping me here,' said Baxter, 'I had nothing to do with the attack.'

'These men you were with,' the superintendent began slowly, ignoring the complaint, 'what was your connection to the assailant?'

'As I told your constables, I don't even know these men. But I would guess they were just a bunch of Rangers' thugs, taking out their anger on the nearest victim.'

'I'm not asking for your speculation. And what are you trying to say, that all Rangers supporters are thugs?'

'No, just this lot.'

Middlemiss peered at Baxter as though he was in a very poor light.

'You know what *I* think. I think you do know these men. I think you do were involved in the attack.'

'Only in that…'

'Only in that what?'

'Only in that I knew the victim. And that I was trying to protect him.'

'Really? So you're a hero then, is that it?'

'No, not at all. I was just trying to help a pal.'

'So how are you acquainted,' he looked down at his notepad, 'with Mister Zogalla? Funny name that. What is it, Italian?'

'German. I used to buy smokes at his tobacco shop on my way home from work. We struck up a friendship. Sometimes I stayed back for a chat.'

'Stayed back for a chat,' mused Middlemiss. 'Isn't that nice. And what did you talk about?'

'Nothing out of the ordinary. Just everyday stuff… our

families, work, the war.'

'The war? Really?'

Middlemiss took another sip from his mug.

'These "Rangers thugs", as you call them. We've had our eye on some of these gangs. We have reason to believe that many of them are affiliated with the Communist Party. So what were you doing in the company of Communist sympathisers?'

'I'm not a Commie. I was just trying to protect the tobacconist.'

'Oh? So fraternising with a Nazi sympathiser as well. You're mixing with the wrong crowds, James Baxter. It wouldn't surprise me if you were anti Semite into the bargain. Did you know that many of the pillars of Glasgow society are from the Jewish community?'

Baxter remained silent.

'Well?'

Baxter assured the superintendent that he was neither a communist nor a Nazi sympathiser. Nor anti Semite.

'I think I should inform you, given that you were such great chums with the victim and all, that he died from his wounds this afternoon. He was taken to the Victoria Infirmary, but the doctors were unable to revive him.'

'Dear God.'

'He may have died when his head hit the curb,' continued the superintendent. 'That makes it aggravated manslaughter. Or he may have died from the boots of one of his assailants. That makes it murder. We'll know after the autopsy. So you can see, either way your pals are in a bit of bother.'

'They're not my pals.'

'So you said... It's just that one of the constables got sight of a couple of them as they were fleeing the scene. He recognised them as some bad lads from the Plantation district, just over the road from where you live, as a matter of fact. So you're sure none of the faces ring any bells?'

'The only thing ringing was my ears when they thumped me.'

'You're quite the comedian James Baxter.'

Middlemiss tapped his forehead with his index finger. 'So when that headache of yours clears and, just perhaps, you suddenly remember something, give me a call. Look, we just need a name. OK?'

The Superintendent handed Baxter a card with a phone number on it.

'Fortunately for you, we have a witness who appears to back up your version of events. But don't think we're going to forget about you. You're not in the clear yet, not by a long shot.'

Relieved by the prospect that he might be about to be released, Baxter relaxed a little and took in his surroundings. He spied a bookshelf nailed to the wall behind the superintendent's desk, crammed with titles. It appeared to be made up of exclusively Scottish authors: Sir Walter Scott, Robert Louis Stevenson, Kenneth Grahame, H. Kingsley Long – and a weighty-looking, leather-bound tome at the centre of the collection, *The Complete Works of Robert Burns*.

'None of your English twaddle here,' said Middlemiss, noticing the direction of Baxter's gaze. 'Are you a fan of Rabbie Burns by any chance?'

'Me? Oh aye. Everyone is.' said Baxter, caught off guard by the question.

'You'd be surprised.' Middlemiss knew of at least one chief superintendent in Edinburgh who was less than complimentary. He drained the last of his coffee mug, swung back in his chair and reached up and grabbed the book in question.

'This one's a beauty.'

Middlemiss began to flick through the pages.

'Here's my favourite. Do you mind if I read a little of it?'

'Eh? Oh sure.' Baxter was incredulous, but he thought it best to humour the man who was in a position to charge him with murder. The superintendent's mood had suddenly and inexplicably brightened. So much so that Baxter wondered if it was some sort of trap. Middlemiss was a veritable one-man bad-cop-good-cop routine – a regular Jekyll-and-Hyde, to borrow from Robert Louis Stevenson.

He thought Middlemiss was just going to read in his head, but he suddenly began to recite:

To a Louse

Ha! whare ye gaun' ye crowlin ferlie?

Your impudence protects you sairly…

Baxter thought Middlemiss would stop after the verse but he kept going. After each stanza, he would look up at Baxter as if expecting his rapt attention. At one point a constable appeared at the window in the door, only for the superintendent to wave him furiously away. Baxter squirmed in his chair. Beaten, accused, grieving and in a state of extreme disorientation he was now forced to endure this bizarre display.

O wad some Power the giftie gie us

To see oursels as ithers see us…

Finally, Middlemiss was finished and paused for effect. Baxter wasn't sure whether he was expected to clap or cheer or what.

'That was terrific,' he finally managed.

'You can't beat a little of Scotland's finest poet,' said Middlemiss, a pleased gleam in his eye.

'Well,' said Middlemiss, 'I don't need to keep you any longer. You can be on your way. But don't forget,' he added, suddenly reverting to type with a wagging finger, 'If something comes to mind, let us know.'

As Baxter rose to leave there was a sharp pain in his ribs, making him wince.

'Do you need to go to the infirmary?' offered the superintendent, 'I can send a constable to accompany you.'

'I'll be fine on my own.'

'Aye, you're a Govanhill man right enough, independent. I like that about Govanhill folk. I grew up there myself. I'd like to get back there sometime.'

'Why would you bother?' thought Baxter. *'I'd like to get the hell out.'*

14

=====

A DINNER GUEST

Baxter sustained three fractured ribs during his ill-fated defence of Zogalla. He had been warned by his doctor to stay out of the boxing ring for at least six weeks or he'd 'end up with worse than a few cracked ribs.' But he had no intention of this stopping him from keeping in shape. Baxter had a pair of steel wire stretch cables with a stirrup at each end. He put one around each foot and the other around his hands. Then he extended the cable under tension to work out his chest muscles and biceps – the perfect exercise device in a confined Glasgow flat. Since his enforced layoff from boxing he had upped the ante with the stretch cables to compensate. He was down to his pants and singlet at the end of a vigorous session when there was a knock at the door. The oldest Baxter sibling, Gregor, answered the door to reveal his father's new-found friend Colin McAllister.

'Hello son. Is your father home?'

'You caught me by surprise,' said Baxter, puffing heavily as he put aside his stretch cables, 'you're a little early.'

'Please, don't let me interrupt,' said Colin.

But secretly Baxter was pleased. He didn't mind showing off

his build to other men – making up for the absence of a father with the demonstration of his physical prowess.

Colin smiled inwardly, he too was feeling unaccountably pleased. 'He's got the brawn but I've got the means,' he thought.

'That'll do me,' said Baxter, 'I've done my quota of presses for the day. Doctor's orders. I've got to stay away from physical sports until my ribs heal.'

'Is that our guest arrived?' called out Jude from the kitchen.

'Dinner will be ready in twenty minutes,' she added. 'I hope you like Irish stew.' But she didn't emerge from the kitchen.

'Dreadful business with the tobacconist,' said Colin. 'You're quite the hero.'

'Me? No really. The police were far from impressed. They seem to think I'm involved. It's giving me a few sleepless nights I can tell you,' said Baxter, gesturing for Colin to take a seat at the dining room table. In an unfortunate faux pas, Colin ended up at the head of the table. He made to get up and take an adjoining seat but Baxter waved it away as a frivolity.

'Have the police any leads yet?'

Baxter cleared his throat. 'Well… not that I know of. It was all fists and boots from a drunken gang. They'll have their work cut out.'

The identity of the assailant he recognised weighed heavily on Baxter. He could easily have given the police a name – Middlemiss had surely suspected as much – but it was absolutely outside the code of the streets, so he had remained silent. Baxter convinced himself that Willie had been at the periphery of the mob and not involved directly in the assault. Plus, he had a more compelling reason to remain schtum. Willie was a crony of Wee Alec's. He didn't want to cross the gang leader.

63

Still, an innocent man had been battered to death. And for what? Nothing more than being the wrong nationality in the wrong place. An outlet of rage for a gang over something as inconsequential as the loss of a football match. Rangers losing to Celtic was serious but not *this* fucking serious. Also, Baxter had lost a friend. He deeply missed the level-headed German and their afternoon chats. A blossoming friendship cut brutally short. Zogalla's death was utterly senseless. Here was a man who had lost everything: his country, his family and now his life – when all he wanted to do was live out his days quietly out of harm's way. But harm had found him. The whole tragic incident had left him deeply conflicted.

The two Baxter boys, Gregor and Billy, crowded around the table. They didn't get many dinner guests and they had no intention of letting this one go without a grilling.

'Who's your football team?' demanded Billy.

'Well, I've been to a few Third Lanark games with your father. Maybe I'll support them.'

'My pa's a boxer,' boasted Gregor. 'He's never lost a fight.'

'That's not quite true son. I've never been knocked out.'

'Are you a boxer?' said Billy.

'Well, no.'

'What do you do?'

'I sell paintings.'

'Do you paint them?'

'No, just sell them.'

'Oh.'

The boys seemed a little disappointed. Hazel emerged from the kitchen with a plate of thickly buttered slices of bread. She smiled coquettishly at the stranger, who gave her a wink, and returned to the kitchen to help her mother.

'Right you two, that's enough. Stop harassing our guest. Go and wash your hands the pair of you – dinner's almost ready,' said Baxter.

After a curt hello, Jude ignored their dinner guest to the point of rudeness. It was only near the end of the meal, it seemed to Baxter, that she warmed to him. The Baxter boys wolfed down their dinner – their appetites sharpened by a game of street football with other boys from the tenements – and drifted away from the dinner table. Hazel trailed after them.

'The two of you really must come to my gallery,' said Colin mopping up the last of his Irish stew with a slice of bread.

'I don't know about that,' protested Jude, 'I'm sure I'd be totally out of my depth surrounded by all those fine paintings.'

'Nonsense,' said Colin. 'My compliments on the dinner by the way – that was delicious.'

'It's an old recipe from my aunt in Ireland. 'I stayed there during the war. I was only a girl, you see.'

'You still are.'

'Oh Colin, please,' she replied, unable to suppress a smile.

Jude looked quickly over at her husband, who kept his head over his plate and said nothing.

'And how about yourself Jimmy. Did you see any action during the war?'

'Well no,' said Baxter shifting in his chair. 'I was stationed here in Glasgow, helping to build the bombers.'

'And how did that sit with you?' said Colin. 'Staying back in Glasgow while most of our boys were on the frontline.'

'Not too well I can tell you,' replied Baxter gruffly. 'But I did what I had to do.'

'Well,' said Colin with a smile. 'In the service of the Royal Airforce. I suppose that makes you quite the hero.'

It was not the first time in their short acquaintance that Baxter had seen that smile, but he couldn't quite get a read on it. It seemed friendly enough but he couldn't quite shake the feeling that he was being mocked. But he dismissed this as not having the same breeding as a man as well-educated and well-spoken as Colin. Best to take him at face value, thought Baxter.

'And what did you do during the war Mister McAllister?' asked Jude.

'Oh well, I wasn't considered for active service after I wrecked my back during a rock climbing accident on Ben Nevis.' Baxter wanted to ask which part of Ben Nevis you could rock-climb. He didn't know of any but refrained from asking this delicate question of a guest.

'Yes my doctor was quite concerned for my well-being for a while there,' continued Colin. 'There were concerns I'd need a walking stick for the rest of my life. But as you can see I've been very lucky – I've made a full recovery. The advances in modern-day medical science have been quite incredible.'

'Right enough,' said Baxter.

'Good to hear you've recovered,' said Jude. 'How about some dessert. Would care for a little trifle?'

'I'd love some.'

Later that night in the matrimonial bedroom, Jude was fretting over the embarrassment of bringing a dinner guest to their modest lodgings.

'It's such a pokey wee flat,' she said, 'I'm sure he's used to being in much grander surroundings.'

'He seemed to enjoy himself well enough,' countered Baxter.

'Well he did that,' she conceded. 'But he doesn't seem very respectful of you.'

'How do you mean?'

'Have you not noticed the way he flirts with me?'

Baxter chewed this over for a moment. 'That's just his way,' he said, dismissing the charm as a harmless quirk of the educated classes. 'He means nothing by it.'

Jude stared at the back of her husband, wondering what could possibly be going through his head. But he kept his face over his cryptic crossword, as if in a state of deep concentration, and remained silent.

15

=====

THE GALLERY

Jude checked the signage to make sure she had the right place. *Prestige Art,* boasted the placard over the entrance in a bold flourish. White on a black background, just like his business card. Jude found herself in a foyer with a number of paintings on the wall – mostly in an abstract style – of which she could make little sense. Jude felt a catch in her throat. She was suddenly nervous. She had noticed that Colin's art gallery was quite close to where she worked and after she finished for the day at the doctor's surgery she began walking absently in the general direction of the gallery until she found herself in front of it.

I must be mad coming here, she thought to herself. And then she went right in. A girl stood behind a greeting desk and took in Jude's appearance with a disapproving gaze.

'Can I help you?' enquired the girl. She was pretty. About twenty. With a striking head of bouncy flaming red hair, making Jude feel all of her thirty-one years. The girl appeared to be attired in some sort of uniform. Smart blue blazer and skirt and a starched white blouse. Jude cursed inwardly that she had not taken greater care of her outfit, dressed as she was in her receptionist's uniform, fresh from the doctor's surgery. Still, she knew the dress showed off her full figure to good effect. But now she wasn't so sure. The fresh-faced beauty of the girl caught her off guard.

'Is Mister McAllister in?'

'Oh aye, I'll just get him for you,' said the girl in a lilting east-coast accent. 'Who should I say is calling?'

'Jude Baxter.'

The girl trotted nimbly over to a staircase leading upstairs.

'Colin,' she called out. 'There's a customer here to see you. A Missus Baxter?'

Precocious little hussy, thought Jude, referring to me as "missus".

The women shared a few awkward moments until Colin came bounding down the stairs towards them.

'So you *did* come,' he said. His bearing and deep confident voice seemed to fill the room.

'Yes, that painting you were talking about,' she said, suddenly becoming very formal, 'by that French painter... of the two Tahitian girls? I'd like to see it.'

'Of course, let me show you. It's upstairs.'

Colin guided her up the stairs to the first floor. With a twinge of unease, she felt his hand resting lightly on the small of her back.

'Yes, that painting is by the French master Paul Gauguin entitled *Two Tahitian Lovelies*. We're very fortunate to have it. It's creating quite a stir among our most discerning art-lovers I can tell you.'

Then as they moved out of earshot, his tone became more confidential.

'Oh Jude, I'm so glad you've come.'

'Well you know, I was just on my way home from my work –

and I thought I'd just pop in.'

'You're looking well,' said Colin as they reached the top of the stairs, gazing intently into her eyes. Jude picked awkwardly at the clasp of her handbag but said nothing. Apart from a few prospective buyers wandering about the gallery, they had the floor to themselves.

'Right then,' said Colin, 'How about I give you a guided tour then–' Jude nodded her approval '– starting with the fine work of Monsieur Gauguin.'

Jude stood in front of the work and tried to make sense of it. Even to her untrained eye, the bold use of colour was exquisite. The artist's interpretation seemed to present a fresh take on the world.

'His paintings are creating quite a stir in Paris and London. A heap of his works were discovered in a hut in Tahiti and more have been found since – it's one of the most important discoveries of impressionist art ever made. And the value of Gauguin's work is increasing every day – I've been lucky enough to have secured this piece for the gallery. It's due to go up for auction next month.'

'Are all his paintings of Tahitian models?' asked Jude.

'Not exactly. But you didn't come here just to look at paintings, I hope.'

Jude felt Colin's urgent presence and his gaze upon her but kept her eyes on the painting. She experienced excitement growing within her but tried to contain it.

'Perhaps you can show me the rest of the gallery,' she suggested.

Any chance of intimacy was undermined by the presence of an art connoisseur who kept badgering Colin questions about his possible acquisitions.

'I've got some business to attend to near Govan,' said Colin. 'I can catch the tram across with you if you like. And anyway it's not always safe for a girl in this part of Glasgow.'

'I'm a big girl, Mister McAllister. I can look after myself. But I suppose if you're heading that way anyway…'

Colin gave his receptionist some final instructions while Jude waited diplomatically near the entrance.

'Right. I'll leave it with you Sheila. If anyone phones about the Paul Gauguin painting, get their details – I'll deal with it personally tomorrow.'

'I'll make sure of it.'

Jude noticed the girl's gaze lingering on Colin as they left; She surprised herself with a pang of jealousy.

Jude offered Colin a cigarette while they waited for the tram.

'Who's the girl?' she asked.

'Sheila? My receptionist. She's been with me about two months now.'

'Attractive.'

'Aye, she's quite a pretty little lass at that. But she's not in your league Judith Baxter.'

He took a puff of his cigarette and blew out the smoke to the sky.

'You're quite a woman. You can act. You can sing – you can even make Irish stew.'

'Honestly, what are you like,' she said, unable to keep the pleasure out of her voice.

He gave a deep, warm laugh that seemed to rumble from within him.

The tram came into view, squeaking in protest as it made a right-angle turn out of Cathcart Road into their street. The tram was painted in an improbable orange-and-green colour scheme. Possibly in an attempt to brighten up the surroundings. Or maybe as a way of appeasing both of the city's largest religious denominations. Colin paid for them both and ushered them up to the top deck – it was draughtier than downstairs but it had the advantage of a greater degree of privacy.

Sitting side by side in the narrow tram seats, she felt their legs pressed together but did not draw away.

'You know,' confided Colin, 'I didn't think you liked me much when we first met.'

He looked uncertainly into her eyes and it occurred to her that maybe he wasn't quite as invulnerable as he appeared. The thought excited her.

'But maybe you're warming to me a little?'

'Impress me,' she said, with a playful smile.

16

UP THE HI-HI!

The city of Glasgow was abuzz. Real Madrid had just defeated Eintracht Frankfurt 7-3 to win the European Cup Final at Hampden in front of 135,000 spectators. The football played that day was exquisite in its attacking nature, the likes of which had rarely been seen in Scotland. Games in the Scottish FA were typically stoic, defensive affairs with score-lines typically 0-0 or 1-0. But this scintillating football fired the imagination of all who witnessed it.

That Glasgow was at fever pitch over a game of football was hardly unusual – do-or-die encounters between Rangers and Celtic often fired the city's collective consciousness. Sport being an escape for many in a city with such long, drab winters.

But there was a particular family in Govan who were working themselves up into a frenzy over a football match. And it didn't involve Real Madrid. Nor Rangers. Nor Celtic. For the Baxter clan at 29 Govanhill Street were staunch supporters of Third Lanark, the *other* Glasgow team of the day, and they were having a season like no other. Modest, unfancied Thirds – the Hi-Hi to their loyal fans – were sitting high on the Scottish table, just behind their

Old Firm rivals. They had thrilled the local football scene with their own scintillating brand of play, which delighted Thirds fans and neutrals alike. Incredibly, with one game to go in the season, they had scored ninety-four goals and had a realistic (albeit slim) opportunity to become the first team in Scottish football history to score 100 goals in a season. Not even the mighty Rangers or Celtic had achieved that.

It was largely down to the extraordinary efforts of the club's front three: Hilley, Harley and Gray. Each was having seasons that surpassed their earlier efforts. At times, they seemed to have almost a telepathic understanding of each other. They clicked in such a way to produce irresistible, creative football – and lots and lots of goals. Thirds' game plan that year was built around all-out attack. And if the opposition managed to put a few goals past them, it didn't matter as long as Hilley-Harley-and-Gray combined to score three, four, or even five goals to secure victory for their team. They formed one of the most lethal – and entertaining – combinations ever seen in the annals of Scottish football.

It was a typical cold and sunless Saturday afternoon as Baxter and his two boys trooped out of the close of their tenement building and made the short twenty-minute walk to Cathkin Park to watch their beloved Thirds for the final game of the season – and the hope of seeing them pull off something special. Hazel had been packed off to her gran's for the day. Her presence not considered appropriate for such an auspicious match. Jude expressed very little interest in football, so she too was exempt.

The three Baxter boys made their way expectantly along Hollybrook Street, with other supporters heading for the ground. As the stadium came into view, the anticipation of the swelling crowd could be heard, as good-natured cheers and whistles rang out.

'Just think,' said Gregor, 'it will just take a hat-trick from Harley and a goal or two from Hilley and Grey… we can get the six goals we need.'

'Aye,' added Billy, 'And if Goodfellow and McInnes can nab a couple… we can win 10-nil!'

'Don't get too carried away,' chastised his older brother, 'we just need six goals, not ten.'

Baxter senior also felt his son's excitement but tried to prick the balloon of their enthusiasm with a little healthy scepticism.

'Don't get your hopes up. We'll have to play at our best to put six past this lot.'

They reached the ground. Baxter bought one adult and one child ticket for Gregor. Billy got in for free as his father was able to carry him over the turnstiles. They took up their usual positions on the northern flank – standing room only. There was limited seating in the stand but the atmosphere was better here, the banter more entertaining. And with a commanding view of the goalmouth action at both ends. Baxter had never seen the ground so packed. Or the atmosphere so tense. By his estimate, there must have been in excess of 10,000 fans.

Baxter's scepticism about the game was well founded. Thirds' opponent for the day was Hibernian, an Edinburgh team known for its tough defence. As part of their back four, Hibs had recruited two from the Gorbals, notorious hard men, who boasted that they would knock the cheeky wee Protestant gobshites into Proddy heaven – notably Messrs Hilley-Harley-and-Gray. The Hibs players emerged onto the pitch first, attired in green shirts and white shorts. They were greeted with jeers.

Then there was a resounding roar, as out came the Thirds players, sporting their traditional red shirts with white collars. It was a clash in every sense of the word, a clash of colours, cities, football styles and Christian denominations.

A hush descended as the referee blew for kick-off. For all their huffing and puffing, the Hibs back four were barely able to lay a boot on the home team's celebrated trio. The Thirds forwards were on fire, putting three goals past the dour Hibs defence in the first twenty minutes. There was a gasp from the stands just before half time when Harley was hacked down in the penalty area by a savage tackle as he made a mesmerising run towards goal. But he got to his feet unhurt and took the penalty kick himself, calmly rolling the ball past the keeper. Four-nil to Thirds!

The mood in the crowd at half-time was rapturous, the hubbub of voices speculating on what could unfold in the second half. The crowd began to sing snatches of songs, a chant broke out among the spectators, directed at the small knot of Hibs supporters who had bravely made the trip from Edinburgh:

As we were passing Cathkin
We heard the mighty roar
Thirds beating Hibs
A hundred goals to four
The ball was in the centre
The ball was in the net
And wee Willie Johnstone
Was sitting in the wet!

The second half began as brightly as the first with Thirds adding a fifth goal just after the restart. When Hibs pulled one back a few minutes the mood remained buoyant. With almost an entire half to go, it seemed inevitable that Thirds would register its hundredth goal for the season.

But then things began to wrong. The Thirds forwards failed to put away a couple of golden opportunities. Gray sent a thunderous free kick against the Hibs crossbar, which then rebounded harmlessly away. Then, with Hilley bearing down on goal with only the Hibs keeper to beat, the linesman raised his flag for offside – met with howls of protest from the Thirds faithful.

'Get the hair out your eyes, ref!' shouted out one wag near Baxter and the boys to the bald-headed official who made the call.

As the game wore on the crowd began to mutter with unease. As the seconds ticked by, goal-scoring opportunities seemed to dry up. With just five minutes to go, it seems as if Thirds would end the season marooned on 99 goals. Then, with moments to spare, Hilley split two defenders with a pass, Harley outsprinted his opponents and hit a perfectly weighted cross from the touch line, looping over the head of the goalkeeper and last defender onto the waiting head of Gray, who thumped the ball into the back of the net – and Cathkin erupted. Ten thousand fans sounded like 60,000. Delirious fans shouted and danced. Perfect strangers embraced. Gregor and Billy jump all over their father. In a rare show of affection, Baxter responded – putting his arms around both of the boys and lifting them off the ground in an enormous bear hug – totally forgetting about his cracked ribs. So deafening was the noise among the crowd that when the referee blew the final whistle, it was all but drowned out. Final score: Third Lanark 6, Hibernian 1.

As the spectators streamed out of the stadium, Baxter fancied a celebratory pint at the Hi Hi Bar. But given the prevailing excitement and the establishment's proximity to the Gorbals, the chance of trouble was likely. Plus, he wanted to stay with the boys and bask in the glow of Thirds' famous victory.

They arrived back home triumphantly and noisily the boys eager to tell their mother all about it, but Jude was still out – presumably doing a shift at the doctor's surgery – so Baxter decided to make tea for the boys, a humble repast of fish fingers and chips. Vegetables were not a notable feature of meals in Glasgow at the time. Baxter turned on the chip fryer and peeled and sliced the potatoes. All the while Gregor and Billy bantered a play-by-play about each of Thirds' six goals and argued about which was best.

Baxter dropped the chips into the heated oil of the chip fryer, accompanied by a cacophonous sizzle.

'You can hear the sound of the Hampden roar!' he exclaimed.

'Surely you mean the Cathkin roar,' corrected Gregor. 'I've never heard anything like it.'

'Aye son, today was 10,000. But just imagine the noise with 100,000 at Hampden – and Scotland putting six of the best past England.'

'But England always beat us,' said Billy miserably.

'Not every time. We've beaten the English before and we'll beat them again. Especially if we play Hilley-Harley-and-Grey up front.'

'They'll never get selected for Scotland,' said Gregor, 'there's a conspiracy against Thirds players.'

'Well, they'll have to get a game after today. Right you two, time for your tea.'

Baxter put down four plates of food, expecting Jude to be home at any moment. Baxter put a liberal dollop of HP Sauce on the side of his plate but didn't bother to ask the boys – they had tried it once and expressed undying dislike of the stuff. After they finished their meal, Baxter put Jude's plate in the oven to keep it warm. Where could she be, he wondered. Still not home at this hour.

After Baxter sent the boys to bed, he completed the entirety of the *Glasgow Herald* cryptic crossword. Like his sons, he too was reliving the afternoon's incredible football match but at the back of his mind, something continued to worm away uneasily. Where was Jude?

About midnight Billy wandered out in his pyjamas.

'Is mammy back yet?' he asked.

'Never you mind son, get away back to your bed.'

'I can wait with you,' said Billy.

'Do you want to feel the weight of my hand?' snapped his father. 'Get back to bed. Now.'

Billy retreated to the kitchen alcove and the safety of his bunk.

17

=====

BOXING DAY

Some years back, when I still had hopes. When I dreamed of being something more than a person living alone in a bedsit in one of the less-fashionable parts of Melbourne, my family used to hold an annual Boxing Day get-together. This usually took the form of a barbeque. This was in sharp contrast to a Scottish Christmas celebration, held cosily indoors in the depths of a sleety, sub-freezing British winter, tucking into traditional yuletide fare with a "wee dram" of something or other. Christmas in the southern hemisphere tended to be rambling affairs, sprawling over several days in an outdoor setting. Typically with the first of the summer heatwaves well under way. Traditional offerings such as turkey, ham and plum pudding were spurned for less formal fare such as lamb chops, sausages, onions, bread, a token salad and Victoria Bitter beer. Or for those living high on the hog, chilled white wine and champagne. And a feast of seafood lobster prawns and mussels, giving rise to that accursed antipodean expression 'throw another prawn on the barbie'.

My brother's Boxing Day barbeque proved no exception. As he had the largest house, it was natural for the festivities to be held there. It was the one time of the year that the extended family got together – and usually a recalcitrant blow-in or two besides. Notable among these special guests was Aunty Mary the Naughty Fairy, who seemed to fly in every year from Scotland, just for our family gathering and to delight in the mayhem she created. It was like…

And now, introducing live, all the way from Scotland, flown in no expense spared, by special request...it's…Aunty Mary the Naughty Fairy!

She wasn't really called that of course, but as the purveyor of everything from gossipy family titbits to bombshells, that was the name that stuck in my mind. I wasn't even sure exactly where she fitted into the family tree to be honest – some great aunt of a distant cousin from what I can ascertain – but there she would be on the day after Christmas, holding court on my brother's expansive second-floor balcony, as summer sunshine filtered through the gum trees. She was invariably attired in an extravagant, billowing gaudily-coloured summer dress – tropical birds-patterned was one I recall with horror – and sporting some outrageous new detail of her appearance, such as having her hair blow-waved into an expansive afro, or dyed a particularly egregious shade of purple, which made me wonder if she was the full quid to be honest. But as the day unfolded and she made her incisive pronouncements on the family history it was clear she had all her wits about her.

There was one Boxing Day, in particular, that was more scandalous than the others. The festive imbibing had followed a familiar pattern. We progressed from beer, to wine, to port and –

once the drinkers had reached an advanced state of inebriation –
my sister would up the ante by bringing out her infamous
homemade Baileys Irish Cream. This tended to finish off anyone
who still had pretensions of sobriety.

It was late in the afternoon, when most everyone had reached
that delicious, what-the-hell, I'm-on-holiday stage of inebriation.
As we lounged about on the upstairs balcony, I struck up a
conversation with Aunty Mary. She was enlightening me about
the good old days in Scotland. Other people drifted in and out of
the conversation but it seemed her focus was on me.

'Yes your mother was a fine actress. But she was an even
better singer when she was younger, simply wonderful. When
she was up on that stage and closed your eyes, you'd swear it
was Judy Garland herself,' enthused Aunty Mary.

'Of course, I don't know where she gets it from,' she
continued. 'No-one on your grandmother's side of the family is
musical.'

'She simply adored her father,' I said, 'she used to talk about
him all the time.'

'Interesting you say that,' said Aunty Mary, giving me a
steady eye from under a hedge of coiffured hair. She seemed very
much on the ball, despite having seemed to have consumed as
much alcohol as anyone else.

'You know of course that your grandfather, Tommy Eadie,
went to Canada for a while when he couldn't find work during
the Great Depression in Glasgow.'

I nodded that I had heard something to this effect.

'Well, what you probably don't know is that while he was
away, your grandmother took in a lodger, to help pay the bills
and that. This was just before your mother was born of course.'

She leaned forward slightly, and then in a conspiratorial tone added, 'Your grandmother was very fond of him and all.' Aunty Mary took a sip of her Baileys and remained silent, allowing the significance of the statement to sink in.

'She fell pregnant while Tommy was away in Canada. It would've been quite the scandal I can tell that you, but she did a good job of concealing it.'

I cast my eyes about to see if anyone else had heard this incendiary comment. There was certainly a number of people within earshot, including one of my brothers. Despite Aunty Mary's extraordinary announcement, I seemed I have been the only one to hear. No one reacted in any way. It was bizarre. like in that movie *Ghost*, where the only person that can see the spirit of Sam Wheat is the sham clairvoyant Eva May Brown. Is it possible no one else had heard what she was saying? Or perhaps this was common knowledge to everyone else and they were simply turning a blind eye to Aunty Mary's remarks.

'Your mother was the target of a lot of animosity when she was young, for events not entirely of her own making,' she continued, just as casually as she was discussing items for sale at a school fete.

Aunty Mary had not actually said that Tommy what not the father. But the implication was clear: the man who raised my mother, whom she had adored, was not her father.

Why had she singled me out with news? Maybe she hoping I'd put one and one together... and come up with three. Maybe she was just trying to show me what it was like to walk a mile in someone else's shoes – or to borrow from The Proclaimers, *five hundred* miles. Just to show me how tough my mother had it growing up. And maybe she was right. Maybe so. And maybe we'd all had just one homemade Baileys Irish Cream too many. And imaginations were running wild.

18

=====

DANCEHALL DAYS

'It's a real corker I can tell you,' enthused Colin on the merits of his newly purchased motor car. 'It's got leather seats and everything.'

'You must be doing all right if you can afford a new car,' said Jude.

'It's not quite new, but as good as – only driven to church by a Vicar on Sundays,' he joked. 'I've been lucky, in the right place at the right time. The Glasgow art scene is booming. Art dealers with a discerning eye can make a killing.'

The pair were walking along under Colin's big umbrella. Rain had set in, a persistent, penetrating drizzle. The Scottish spring seemed determined to stay away, but it did little to dampen Jude's spirits. She had finished her shift at the doctor's surgery early, feigning a migraine. She hardly recognised her own behaviour, even a white lie was a big deal for her; her mother would have been mortified at even this modest deception.

They had just shared a meal at a newly-opened Portuguese restaurant, the only one of its kind in Glasgow. Jude had never been in such a fancy establishment and had been suitably overawed.

They approached the entrance of the Kelvingrove Museum.

'It's funny,' said Jude, 'all this time living in this city and I've never been here.'

She leant towards Colin and kissed him lightly on the cheek. Colin crooked his arm and Jude took it. They walked arm in arm into the foyer of the gallery, a grand, gothic-looking interior with an imposing arched ceiling. Even the floor was impressive, comprised of black, white and gold patterned marble. It had been made wet by the day's steady rain and the comings and goings of art lovers with dripping umbrellas. There was a sign at the entrance warning people to be careful not to slip.

It had been Colin's idea to come here. There was an exhibition of Chinese antiquities: Ming dynasty vases, watercolour paintings, statues of emperors and diminutive Jade horses. All purloined from China during European occupation.

Jude barely noticed the artworks. Colin kept her amused with stories from his days at art school and some of the quirks of the eccentric teachers. It had been Colin's idea to visit the museum, but once there his interest seemed to wane.

'A penny for your thoughts,' Jude asked.

'You know what?' said Colin, 'I need to take a break from art this evening.'

'How do you mean?'

'Well, it's Saturday night. There's only one thing for it – let's go dancing.'

Colin watched her face as she swept a lock of hair out of her eyes.

'Where?'

'At the Locarno.'

Jude weighed up the proposal. It was the most stylish

dancehall in all of Glasgow at the time, famous for jiving. And smooching.

'I'm too old for the Locarno.'

'Don't be daft.'

He was close. She took in his scent, recognising it as Old Spice. Such a contrast to her husband. He wouldn't be seen dead doing anything as "pampered" as wearing cologne. When she thought of her husband, the scent that came to mind was grease from the tool shop where he worked.

The Locarno was *the* place to be on a Saturday night in Glasgow. When Colin and Jude arrived there was already a thumping dancefloor full of revellers. Bill Haley and the Comets' *Rock Around the Clock* blared out of the speakers scattered around the venue. Colin got them both a drink and they stood at the end of the dancefloor, acclimatising to the noise and flashing lights. Jude swayed a little to the music and looked on at the mayhem in front of them. The songs came fast and furious. Bill Haley gave way to *Rave On* by Buddy Holly – kicking the song off with his own version of the Glaswegian glottal stop. Then came Jerry Lee Lewis with *Great Balls of Fire*. As he bashed out his rippling piano solo, people started jitterbugging.

'Let's give it a go,' said Colin.

'I don't know this dance step,' said Jude, having seen it but unable to put a name to it.

'Honestly Jude. How is it somebody who loves music as much as you do can't do the jitterbug?'

'If I'm not too old for dancing, I'm *definitely* too old for this,' she said, flicking her head towards the dancers.

'Nonsense.'

Without another word, Colin took her by the hand and led her out to the dance floor.

He tried to teach her the fast staccato moves. She became breathless with laughter while she tried to master the dance step. Colin, of course, was already accomplished. The song gave way to Chuck Berry's *Johnnie B Goode*. Colin abandoned his impromptu jitterbug lesson and they settled into more familiar dance steps.

As the night wound down, less-frenetic numbers came on. The lights dimmed and couples started slow dancing cheek to cheek. As Fats Domino sang *Blueberry Hill*, Jude found her thrill in the arms of her would-be lover.

'Do you want to come back for a night cap?' said Colin, as she swayed to the music. Jude responded by nuzzling into his neck like an affectionate puppy dog.

'I'll take that as a yes.'

When Jude returned home well after midnight her husband was still awake, sitting on their marital bed with a reading lamp on. An open book lay face down on the bedside table. He eyed her suspiciously as she entered.

'Where have you been?' he demanded.

'Didn't I tell you?' she said, with an attempted air of casualness. 'Rita's birthday celebration was on tonight.'

'No.'

'The night got away from us.'

'So that makes it okay does it? Coming home at two a.m., reeking of smoke and alcohol. No explanation. Nothing.'

Baxter glared at her, but she didn't meet her husband's eye.

'It must have been some party.'

'It was. I'm exhausted, I'm going to sleep.'

He was moved to anger by the impudence of her dismissal. But despite the provocation, he did not raise a hand to his wife.

She quickly undressed and got into bed, facing away from him.

'It's just that the boys wanted to see you when they came home tonight,' he said, trying for a gentler tone, 'they wanted to tell all about Third's big win.'

Sport. How typical, she thought. It was all that seemed to matter to him. But now, Jude Baxter had something a good deal more interesting than football to engage her.

Despite her outer bravado she was trembling inside. But not from her husband's eyes boring into her back or even her mother's imagined guilty accusations. The trembling was for the touch of another man, who had shaken her to the core.

19

=====

A WEE BLETHER

'He took us to this fancy Portuguese restaurant. You should have seen it,' enthused Jude to her bosom buddy, Rita. They met at secretarial college several years earlier and had been friends ever since.

'Oh, I'm so envious. What was it called?'
She took a puff of her cigarette and thought for a moment.

'A Lorcha, Il Orcha – something like that.'

Jude was seated at her receptionist's desk at the doctor's surgery. Her boss was in consultation with a certain Missus McCormack, a lady of some standing, notorious for demanding long consultations for her various ailments.

Jude adjusted the phone headset against her ear and continued: 'We started with vegetable soup and this amazing crusty bread. Then baked chicken and French fries for the main course. Although I think "French fries" is just a fancy way of saying "chips", to be honest. The tablecloths were white. Everything was so clean and posh.'

'Uh-huh.'

'And there were these polite Portuguese waiters with these funny wee moustaches, at least I assume they were Portuguese.

And there was this live music, a man playing Spanish guitar. At one point he was serenading us. It was so romantic – I hardly recognised myself. Colin bought me a rose and put it behind my ear.'

There was some noise from the consultation room. Jude looked up but no one emerged.

'Where was I? Oh yes, and then we went dancing at The Locarno.'

'You didn't.'

'Aye, and Colin's a fabulous dancer and all. I felt like I was dancing with Fred Astaire. And then he tried to teach me this fancy new dance step, but I just could'nae get the hang of it. It was such a scream. Colin was the perfect gentleman the whole time.'

'Of course, I did my best to be charming as well. I just smiled innocently and batted my eyelids and nodded whenever he suggested we do something.'

'It's good to know you've still got it girl,' said Rita.

'High, wide and twenty-one,' Jude said, 'that's me.'

'Och you're terrible so you are.'

'Honestly Rita, he *does* make me feel like a girl again.'

'When are you seeing him again?'

'Wednesday.'

'It sounds like you two are becoming quite the item.'

'God, I hope so.'

Jude took a final puff of her cigarette and stubbed it out on the ashtray.

'And what about Jimmy?' said Rita.

There was a long silence down the line while the significance of the question sunk in. The door of the consultation room swung open and the doctor and Missus McCormack emerged, deep in discussion about the patient's gall stones.

'I've got to go,' said Jude, and hung up.

20

=====

A SHIP FACING OUT TO SEA

Baxter stood in front of the bathroom mirror, lathering his face with a brush in preparation for his morning shave and another day's work at Crockatt's. He reflected that things hadn't worked out quite as he'd hoped. His friendship with Colin felt strained. The last few times the three of them had been together hadn't felt right. Baxter was forced to admit that his idea of connecting with Colin as a way of getting Jude into Glasgow's theatrical scene was not succeeding. He also thought about the tobacconist now and then. And his senseless, monstrous death. The pointlessness of Zogalla's death seemed to give life a randomness that Baxter found disconcerting. Also, he missed the affable German. Missed having an outsider to bounce ideas off.

Oddly, Jude had been in an unaccountably good mood. She had a glow about her, an appearance of rude health. Even regular patients at the doctor's clinic remarked on it. Some speculated that she might be pregnant. Even Baxter noticed – reminding him of the vivacious, carefree girl he had known when they first met. Still, he sensed a growing distance between them. He wanted to bridge that gap. Something he never found easy. He decided to take Jude to the teahouse they used to go to when they first met.

She seemed surprised when he suggested it and then, reluctantly it seemed to Baxter, agreed to go the following Saturday morning.

They took up a table next to the window overlooking Pollokshaws Road and ordered the house special – a pot of tea, and a roll and square sausage apiece. The café was cosy, crowded and overheated, compelling people to shed their bulky overcoats after the chill of outside, where a low cloud blanketed the city. There was a satisfying hubbub of chatter, accompanied by the occasional rustle of newspaper as a patron turned the pages of his *Glasgow Herald*.

'Have you heard anything from Colin about the casting agency?' asked Baxter.

She gave him a sharp look, seemingly startled by the question.

'It's just that I've not seen him for a while. I thought he might have mentioned it to you.'

'Heard something about the casting agency? Well, no.'

'Are you disappointed?' said Baxter, 'I know how much it means to you.'

'Me? It's a bit of a long shot anyway. Don't bother yourself about it,' said Jude, surprisingly non-committal about something she wanted so desperately. 'If it happens, it happens.'

Jude felt sorry for him. It was incredibly naïve to believe their three-way friendship could have worked out that way.

The food and drink arrived. Jude took a slurp of tea and a bite out of her roll, the sausage was spicy – just the way she liked it.

'You know, I've been thinking,' said Baxter, munching on his own roll, 'about all those possibilities abroad.'

Jude absent-mindedly drew a smiley face in the condensation on the inside of the window.

'They're crying out for engineers in Australia right now,' he continued.

'I don't know why you tell everyone you're an engineer when you know perfectly well you're just a cutter in a gear shop.'

'Christ Jude, it's just easier that way. Rather than trying to explain everything to people. Anyway, two of the workers from Crockatt's have already left and taken their families to Perth.'

'Perth, on the west coast?'

'Perth, Australia.'

Baxter was becoming frustrated – his wife was oddly distracted, considering the gravity of what he was proposing. She had always been worried about the idea, now she seemed blasé.

'I don't just mean leave Glasgow, I mean leave Scotland altogether,' said Baxter.

Jude recalled the last time they had left Glasgow for a better life. Jimmy had quit his job and they had uprooted the kids – all under six at the time – and taken them off to Tain in the north of Scotland. She stayed at home in their draughty, white-walled cottage (quaint was one way of describing it; Arctic-like was another) looking after the weans while Jimmy took on a job as a forester. They could barely make ends meet. In the end, Jimmy had to resort to stealing potatoes from a local farmer in the dead of night to feed his brood. Jude shuddered at the thought of the Tain experiment. They had lasted six months and then returned dejectedly to Glasgow.

It was supposed to be their salvation but nothing was solved. They had each seen a strength in the other that wasn't there. She was attracted by his gruff, no-nonsense manner, deep voice and powerful build. But there was a gaping hole left by his unknown father, that no amount of muscle could compensate for. This deficiency became apparent in the early months of their marriage. What she had thought was silent strength was actually a deep-rooted insecurity. For his part, he had been attracted by her adventurous nature and charm. And her bravery. The guts to be able to get up in front of a bunch of strangers, acting and singing her heart out. It seemed to be a great deal more ballsy than getting in a boxing ring with some Glasgow tough nut – intent on trying to knock you into the Trossachs. There, all you got was a physical battering. You didn't run the risk of dying emotionally. What he didn't know was that she was driven by her own overwhelming sense of inadequacy. The confidence she appeared to ooze on stage was actually the desire to lose herself, to obliterate the guilt imparted on her by her mother. Whose withering contempt made it perfectly clear throughout her childhood that she had been an accident, and was most definitely *not* wanted.

'Will you at least think about it,' he said, snapping her out of her Tain reverie. 'It could be the new start we need.'
She took a sip of her tea and said nothing.

'Christ Jude, I know it's not been easy these past few years.'

Try the past ten years, she thought.

'I know living in a pokey wee tenement flat is not the life we envisaged. And I know… well, I know I haven't always been the most available of husbands.'

Jude looked into the twitching muscles of his face to see where this was all going.

'I feel at times,' he continued, 'that I've let you down. But unless you've been through it, you can never know exactly what it's like – the stigma of illegitimacy. The shame of growing up without a father. It makes life difficult. You find yourself unable

96

to do things that other men take for granted. To be able to talk to women. To be affectionate.'

'Most men find it difficult to talk to women.'

'I know I've been cold towards you – I never meant to be. I sense a growing distance between us. And it's my fault, I realise that now. I've been inaccessible to you. Like a ship facing out to sea.'

They finished the last of their roll and sausage, and the dregs from the teapot. Baxter became silent, as if his words had left him exhausted. Jude was stunned. She wondered what had prompted this extraordinary outburst. He had never opened up like this before. She felt a kind of tenderness towards him.

'Don't worry,' she said, patting the back of his hand, 'you'll always have Hazel and the boys.'

21

=====

CONSUMMATION

It seemed to Jude to be the most perfect day of her life. Colin
drove them down to the seaside port of Rothesay in his motor car
for a picnic on the coast. The two-hour drive passed in a blur.
Colin kept the windows down to let in the mild sea air. The pair
passed the time smoking and chatting – Colin with one arm
casually on the steering wheel and the other around Jude's waist.
After arriving in Rothesay, they found a secluded spot among
rocks away from the main village and basked in the unexpected
early summer sunshine. Colin had brought along a hamper of
chicken drumsticks, salad and a bottle of champagne. He had the
lion's share of the alcohol but managed to coax the teetotalling
Jude to at least have a small glass. While the seagulls squabbled
and feasted on the remains of the picnic, the lovers feasted on
each other's lips, their bare feet dangling over the edge of the
rocks, the delicious chill of the small waves lapping around their
ankles.

Now, as they lay naked together in the bed back in Colin's
apartment, Jude's contentment deepened. Her lover had dozed
off in a post-coital stupor. but Jude was wide awake – more alive

than she had ever remembered. She sketched around his breastplate with a finger, drawing the outline of his car. He began to stir.

'What sort of car is it you have?'

She hadn't thought to ask until now.

'Hmm?' he said sleepily. 'Oh, the car. Morris Minor. Duck egg blue as a matter of fact. I'm still trying to master the gears. I hope it wasn't too rough a ride.'

'It was delightful. I didn't know there was so much beautiful Scottish coastline.'

She continued to draw on his breastplate. This time a small heart – the outline of which she drew many times – then finished up by drawing an arrow through it.

'But I know so little about you. Tell me all about yourself Colin McAllister.'

'There's not much to tell really. Failed art student at twenty-five, successful art dealer at thirty-eight, lover of Judith Baxter at forty.'

'What about the other women in your life?'

Colin remained silent for a time, as if carefully selecting his words.

'Well, that's a long story.'

'Were you married?'

'I was. For a while – big mistake. What is it they say? Marry in haste, repent at leisure. Her family made quite a stink when we separated I can tell you.'

'What was she like?'

'I'll tell you another time – let's just enjoy the day, OK?'

'And what about that wee trollop at the art gallery,' said Jude, suddenly anxious. 'What about her?'

99

Colin put a finger to her lips. 'Shh, my lovely Jude. Just relax. I'm all yours. Yours and only yours.'

He felt her mouth smiling under the light pressure of his finger.

'Let's not invite all these strange women into our bed,' he joked. 'Tell you what, why don't you sing me a song?'

The performer within her took little encouragement. She sang *Over the Rainbow* in its entirely, but softly, as if she was singing a nursery rhyme to a sleepless child.

'You sing beautifully,' said Colin. 'From the *Wizard of Oz* isn't it?'

'Yes, Judy Garland's a hero of mine. She was just sixteen when she sang it. What a talent.'

Much had been made in the press of the child star's torturous upbringing. Damaged goods. Jude could identify with that.

The same restless energy that drove Jude to act and sing – to seek out attention and approval – had driven her into the arms of another man. A man who, in truth, she hadn't much liked at first. And, she felt, something that would never have happened without the urging of her husband, who had pushed her into Colin's arms. Her dim Govanhill flat seemed a million miles away.

Jude rolled over on her back and luxuriated in the size of Colin's bed, stretching out like a starfish.

'Just look at the size of this bed,' she marvelled. 'I feel like Lady Muck.'

'It's a king size. I'm glad you like it. I might be moving into a new flat and all, if my latest art deal goes through.'

Jude was surprised at this. It was one of the nicest flats she had seen in Glasgow, one from the new block of apartments on Glen Lora Drive, largely the domain of the up-and-comers, with a few bob in their pocket. Colin must be doing very well for himself if he was contemplating a move to something grander.

She rolled back towards him and pressed her body against his – as if unable to bear being separated from him for more than a few moments. Their love was still so new, but Jude could no longer imagine a life without him. She reflected on their first kiss, the recklessness of doing it in her own close. Not only the exhilaration of the act but the thrill of it. Of doing it right under everyone's nose. Almost as if she wanted to be caught. Perhaps it would have made everything easier if they had been.

'Darling, when are we going to be together?' she asked.

'Soon.'

'It doesn't feel right, all this sneaking about behind his back.'

'I know. It's not ideal.'

'I haven't told Jimmy yet. But I think he's beginning to suspect.'

They hardly referred to Jude's husband as anything other than "him". As if the shared guilt of "him" being the one that had brought them together precluded the use of his name. The mention of his name seemed rude and out of place. Jude immediately regretted saying it.

'Don't tell him just yet,' said Colin. 'Let's wait for the right time… I'm going to close a big deal for the purchase of a Renoir. There's a big European buyer who's almost ready to commit – I don't want any unwanted distraction to cock things up.'

Jude nodded slowly. Showing him that on this, and everything else, they were as one.

She put her lips close to his ear. 'I love you,' she said, in a breathless, girlish, Happy-Birthday-Mister-President whisper.

22

=====

KEYS

Dead. I poke and prod for signs of life. Nothing. It's an ill-tempered day. There's a hot northerly blowing, coming down from the continent's vast arid interior, sucking up heat as it goes. Gathering speed and strength until it arrives at my doorstep with the power of a blast furnace. Doors and windows are swinging open and slamming shut. The violence of the gusts seems to distort the space in my bedsit. Almost as if it's expanding and contracting. The vial sits in pride of place on the mantelpiece. It's standing at attention. Ready for action. Time to activate the contents; unleash its potential.

But not here. I have to go to the car.

I try a few more experimental swipes and button presses on my iPhone. Still nothing – not a flicker. I can never get the hang of these devices and the way they require constant attention to keep the batteries charged. Today I'm not even going to bother. I had just wanted a weather forecast, but now even that simple task is beyond it. I drop my iPhone down on the table. Gone are the days you can slam down a phone in a fit of rage. These new smartphones are as fragile as eggs.

Regrets? Fair to say I've had a few. But now, finally, I'm going to do it my way. Time to address what has eaten away at me for so long. But first I have to find the keys. I haven't used the car for ages. When was the last time? A month at least. Fair to say I don't have much need for it most of the time. But today it will serve an important function.

I turn the bedsit upside down but I can't find my car keys. It's not exactly a large space but the location of the keys eludes me. I rifle through draws, scour the litter-strewn floor, search in the pockets of my pants and shirts. Nothing. It's one of those frustrating times when I wish I had someone else here. To help with the search. To lighten the load. A woman.

But here my deficiencies came to the fore. The women I had attempted to form relationships with would, at some point, usually fairly early on, sniff disdainfully as if they didn't quite like the smell of what they were letting themselves in for and quietly leave. Most emphatically in the early "bloom" of youth then again and in the slow descent into middle age – where I could reflect at leisure on just how I had missed the boat when it came to finding a life companion. Mine was a solo cruise.

But it wasn't all gloom. There was a brief time when my earning capacity, confidence and what remained of my youth coincided to unexpectedly leave me flush in the favour of women. However I frittered this away by living the high life and playing the field. When it was over, all I had was the knowledge that I had squandered the love of the one woman I should have stayed with. Such friends I had at the time said as much but what use it is to command a dog with sharp canines not to bite. Or a man who has some currency with women not to pursue them with reckless abandon. My sputtering star waned and soon I was back where I started. With my appeal to women about as powerful as a scrap of cling wrap. As easily brushed off and disposed of. And forgotten about.

But never mind all of that now. It's time.

After a great deal of rummaging around and cursing, I finally find my car keys. They're in a discarded pair of pants underneath a pile of old clothes in the laundry. How did they get there? Doesn't matter. I pick up the vial off the mantelpiece. I expect it to be heavy, but it's surprisingly light. A sudden gust of wind buffets the bedsit. Very carefully, I place the vial inside a doubly-folded handkerchief and enclose it. Believe me, I'm not being too cautious. I absolutely don't want anything to go wrong at this point. Let's just say I feel more comfortable with the double insurance. Or is it double jeopardy? I put the cocooned vial in the inside pocket of my jacket and walk towards the front door.

23

=====

FANCY MAN

Baxter returned home after a night playing snooker with a few of his pals from work. He was surprised to find Jude at home. She was sewing the seat of Billy's school pants at the kitchen table. This wasn't the life he had envisaged for them. Money was tight, too tight to allow the luxury of throwing out holey clothes. Jude was listening to the radio and humming quietly to herself. She had wanted to listen to some of the songs that she danced to with Colin at the Locarno, but all she could find was a radio show celebrating the life and music of Scottish crooner Kenneth McKellar.

'Why don't you put on the overhead light?' said Baxter. 'You're going to go blind trying to sew in this.'

'I don't want to wake the children,' replied Jude. She smelt the whisky on his breath but made no comment.

'Then why have you got the radio on?' he said.

'It's on low. They can't hear it.'

Baxter was exasperated by his wife's logic. And, lately, she seemed to be getting worse, her manner more erratic. Still, she seemed to be able to keep it together sufficiently to be a mother to her children. It was one of the things that had attracted him when they first met, his sense that she would make a good mother – as the other preconceptions about her fell away, it had been one of the few things in their relationship he had been right about.

'Good to see that you remember that you still have children at any rate', said Baxter.

'What do you expect?' she said.

'I expect you to behave like my wife,' he snapped.

Baxter saw her body stiffen at the change in tone, but she didn't look up.

My wife, he thought. He had been cutting gears at work one afternoon earlier in the week when it struck him that Jude was having an affair with Colin. The thought just occurred to him – arriving with the cold clang of truth. Once he saw it, he could not un-see it. Everything suddenly made sense: Jude's unaccountable good health, her late nights and long absences from home – attributed to overtime at the doctor's surgery – and Colin's increasing frostiness towards him and gradual disappearance from his life. Even Jude's migraines, which she had complained about for years, miraculously stopped.

'Please, don't be so melodramatic,' she said.

'That's rich coming from you – the biggest drama queen in all of Glasgow.'

Jude declined to answer. She just continued humming to herself and sewing.

The bottle of whisky Baxter had shared with his colleagues during the snooker game had the effect of loosening his tongue.

'Not away out with your fancy man tonight?'

'And if I was it would be your fault,' said Jude, not missing a beat. 'You practically pushed us together.'

'That's not fair,' said Baxter. 'You know I was trying to do the right thing.'

"What is it they say about hell and good intentions?' she said, with casual cruelty.

They were sparring around the topic that was uppermost in their minds. The word "affair" danced around the room between them like Mohammed Ali in his pomp, taunting an opponent.

"You used to like him well enough,' continued Jude. 'The best of friends, it seemed.'

'Oh aye, he's quite the patter merchant.'

'You've changed your tune. You were full of his praises the first time you introduced us.'

That was before I was aware of his true intentions, thought Baxter. It was on the tip of his tongue to say it but something made him stop. He had narrowly avoided walking into the sucker punch. He sensed Jude was trying to goad him into mentioning Colin and the affair, taking advantage of his inebriated state to bring things to a head. He didn't want to give her the satisfaction.

So he didn't ask the question. He couldn't bring himself to, he wouldn't like what he was going to hear. And what would happen next. There was a growing defiance in her he had never seen before. All the courage he possessed in the boxing ring seemed to desert him in the face of his fractious wife, who was becoming an unknown quantity. The worst kind of opponent.

24

=====

TIP OFF

Another profitable day in the glamorous world of upmarket art dealing had come to an end. Colin sent his staff home, locked up and was in the back office balancing the day's takings. He was about to put on his coat and leave when the phone rang.

'Prestige Art,' he said automatically.

'The jig is up Colin McAllister,' said an unfamiliar voice. 'Alec McManus knows all about your so-called Renoir original. And I can assure you Mister McManus doesn't take kindly to being sold a pup. If I was you I'd watch your back.'

There was a click then the line went dead. Colin felt his guts drop. Alec McManus. Or "Wee Alec" as he was commonly known. The most feared gang leader in all of Glasgow.

Colin cursed his carelessness. He had a suspicion that the Renoir might not have been properly authenticated, but like everyone else involved, he had turned a blind eye. Now his suspicions were confirmed. That the Renoir was most probably a fake; and now the wrong people had found out. It had been something he had become increasingly uncomfortable with. As Britain boomed post war, Glasgow had been swept along – buoyed by the Clyde shipbuilding industry. Those at the top of the food chain suddenly had money for luxuries, such as fine art. In the early years of his art dealership, Colin had always made sure the necessary checks and balances were performed on artworks, giving such assurances to his high-end customers. He had gradually won their trust. But as the Glasgow art scene began to blossom, fewer questions were asked. Clients still had an appetite for art, but demand was getting harder to meet. So corners were cut by those in the industry to bring artworks to market. And while bank balances grew, so too did the incidence of forgeries. Organised crime pricked up its ears to this lucrative business and became involved, wanting their share. But while the money still flowed, everyone was happy. It was the easiest money Colin had ever made and it seemed to be in no-one's interest to give too much scrutiny as expensive works of art changed hands. And he had gotten away with it. Until now.

Colin collapsed back into his chair. He leant forward on his elbows and put his hands to his lips, as if praying. He took several deep breaths and tried to force himself to stay calm and think. But his hands were trembling.

It couldn't have been one of Wee Alec's envoys who left a message, he reasoned, they would have just popped round and dealt with him in person. A little grievous bodily harm, or perhaps something worse. He had never met Wee Alec in person, but the hard man's reputation preceded him. He was known to hand out vicious beatings to anyone who crossed him. And recently events had taken a more sinister turn, with two bodies found floating in the Clyde over the past few months. The *Glasgow Herald* speculated that this was most likely the work of Wee Alec and his crew.

So the person who had issued the warning on the phone must

be someone with his best interest at heart – possibly someone he brokered a good deal for in the past, someone who wanted to alert him to the danger without directly incurring the wrath of Wee Alec and his gang. But this was mere speculation.

Regardless, if the Renoir was a fake, it would only be a matter of time until Wee Alec found out. But how much time did he have. Weeks? Days? Hours?

In truth, Colin had planned to leave Glasgow anyway. He had taken his business about as far as it could go in this relatively small town and he wanted to try his luck in the big smoke of New York. Now, he would have to bring the plan forward. It occurred to him that the phone call could have been from a rival auction house, trying to put the wind up him. It seemed the most likely explanation. Nevertheless, it was time to get out.

Formulating a plan of action relaxed him a little. He gave out a sigh of relief, got up and left the building.

It was a day of buffeting wind and fierce rain squalls. *A typical Scottish summer's day*, Colin thought grimly. The unsettled weather suited his mood. The pavement was still wet from a recent shower and it looked like the heavens could open at any moment. But Colin decided to walk to his flat; he needed to clear his head. And make some quick, sound decisions. He was determined not to be spooked, not to start jumping at shadows. But he did make the concession of going home via the backstreets to avoid being too visible. The pre-dusk gloom made him edgy. The gunmetal sky hung low, as if pressing down.

As Colin walked, he calculated. By his reckoning, it would take him three days to get his affairs in order. He could let Sheila take over the running of the art gallery. Some of his more saleable artworks he could palm off to some of his rivals. They would undoubtedly bargain him down to the sorts of prices that would represent grand theft but he really had no choice. Plus, he needed some start-up cash for when he arrived in New York. He could crate across some of the remaining artworks to give him a starting portfolio. Just to be on the safe side, he wouldn't leave a forwarding address until … Jude! Following the jolt of the phone call, she had completely slipped from his mind. He was tempted to simply leave for the US and telephone her to explain when he got there but, really, he had no idea when he would be returning to Glasgow.

Reluctantly, he decided that he would have to see her before he left. It was a risk to delay his departure but it couldn't be helped – she had earned her little scene.

25

=====

HEART TO HEART

Baxter opened the door of his Govanhill flat to find all three of his children home, playing cards at the kitchen table. There was no sign of Jude.

'Where's your mammy?' he asked.

'She's away at Granny Eadie's,' said Gregor, not looking up from his hand.

'We're playing Gin Rummy,' added Billy.

'Where did you learn to play that?'

'Tommy at school taught us. His uncle's been to America,' said Gregor.

'But Hazel still disnae know the rules. Do you want to play?' said Billy.

'I do to,' said Hazel indignantly.

She smiled coquettishly as she peered at her cards in a show of studied concentration.

'I'm just back from work,' said Baxter. 'I need a moment's peace.'

Baxter dropped his work satchel on the small table next to the front door and walked across to the couch with the evening edition of *The Glasgow Herald* tucked under his arm. He sat down with a grunt.

'Have you lot had your tea?'

'Mammy made us stovies before she left,' said Gregor. 'Yours is in the oven. Can we have a fish supper tomorrow night?'

'We'll see,' said his father.

Baxter was mindful that it was Thursday and he was all but certain to pop by the chippy on his way home from work on Friday. But he liked to keep them in suspense and then surprise them all – arriving home with the treat, amid a waft of battered fish, chips, vinegar and soggy paper.

Baxter unfolded his newspaper and perused the front-page headlines for the latest on the apprentice welders' strike in the Clyde shipbuilders' dispute.

'Gin,' said Gregor, coolly laying down his cards with a flourish.

'I'm fed up with this,' said Billy. 'Let's go away outside and play fitba instead.'

Playing street football with their pals was a popular after-school pastime of the boys in Glasgow, and Govanhill Street was no exception.

'You're just a sore loser,' said Gregor. 'All right then. Let's go.'

The boys got up from the table and made their way to the front door.

'I'm going to be Harley. You can be Hilley,' said Billy, referring to two of the stars from Third Lanark, the football team they supported.

'No way! *I'm* going to be Harley,' said Gregor.

'Get away. You're no good enough.'

'Put on your jackets before you go out,' said Baxter.

'Och come on, it's no cold,' protested Billy.

'OK then. But make sure you're back before it's dark.'

As the boys left the door slammed shut behind them, their voices fading as they made their way down the stairs.

Hazel sidled over to her father, sat next to him and pressed her face into his bicep. As ever, the smell of grease on his work dungarees giving her a sense of security. Baxter was craving a smoke before his tea, but didn't want to shoo away his daughter. They rarely had time in the flat together. The packet of cigarettes in his pocket could wait. He could see the top of her head over his newspaper. She had her mother's auburn curls.

'What are you readin'?' she asked.

'The workers on the Clyde have gone on strike for more money.'

'What does "strike" mean?'

'They down tools and stop working. Until the boss agrees to pay them more money.'

'But if they stop working, how can they get money?'

Hazel lifted her head and tried to read the headline on the front page of the newspaper.

WELDERS STRIKE ENTERS THIRD WEEK, TRAFFIC DISRUPTED it trumpeted. It was as incomprehensible to her as her father's explanation.

'If they stop working on the ships, there's no one to build them. And then nobody gets paid,' explained Baxter.

'Oh,' she said, nodding her head, but still not really understanding.

'Tell me about the war,' she said. 'Tell me about Dougie again.'

Hazel loved her father's wartime stories of the adventures with his pals, and Dougie was her favourite. She'd had quite enough of the grown-up world of ships and strikes, thank you very much.

Her head was full of their stories. How they would try to outsmart the foreman at the plane factory and sneak out to smoke a cigarette. Or how they were on the bus taking their football team for a game in the north of Scotland and the driver would get lost and Dougie would make everyone laugh by doing impersonations of the coach, when he was out of earshot of course, for he had a fearful temper. But by far the scariest, and most fascinating story, was the time they got bombed.

'Aye well, it started off as a beautiful evening,' said Baxter, recounting the fateful first night of the Clydebank Blitz. 'Me and Dougie had bunked off outside for a wee smoke. And even though all the street lights were turned off because of the war, there was a full moon, making it almost as bright as daytime. It was surreal.'

Hazel sat still, listening with rapt attention.

'We'd barely taken our first puffs when there was a blinding flash and then a sound like thunder, but louder than any thunder you could ever imagine. And not a cloud in the sky. It was then we realised we were being attacked. German planes were dropping bombs on us!'

'But why?' piped up Hazel.

'Britain was at war with Germany. That's what happens during war.'

'But they're not trying to bomb us now.'

'Well no, we've made up of differences.'

'Oh. Is that like making friends again?'

'Something like that. So anyway, the foreman suddenly appeared through a side door. He spoke to us, but it was so loud we could hardly hear him …'

Baxter continued his story, describing the terrible night to his daughter. The scream of air-raid sirens. The explosions. The planes. The return of Scottish artillery fire. Of tenements ablaze and the Clyde River itself, seemingly on fire. And of people left homeless. But he spared his daughter the gorier things he saw that night. The blood. And the awful death toll.

He then went on to describe how he and Dougie had decided to become soldiers and join the British infantry. But that only Dougie had been accepted, to Baxter's bitter disappointment. And what a hero his pal had been, fearless and brave, fighting the enemy on the battlefield. And then how Dougie had met a French lass while on leave during a break in the fighting. And how they had fallen in love, and married, and moved to Canada together. Hazel had heard the story many times before, but never tired of it.

Not the real ending, of course. The unsavoury truth that Dougie had died of dysentery as a prisoner-of-war at the hands of the Japanese was not revealed. Baxter could shield his daughter from that at least.

'And you never saw Dougie again?' said Hazel.

'That's right.'

'You must miss him.'

'Oh aye. But if it wasn't for Dougie, I would never have met your mother. It was his idea that I ask her out on a date.'

Hazel giggled a little at the thought.

'Do you love mammy?' she asked suddenly.

Baxter wondered where his daughter had come up with such girlish notions. He remembered that she had been reading a tattered copy of *Grimms' Fairy Tales* that morning but he couldn't recall any of the fables being about love.

Baxter cleared his throat before he spoke.

'Oh aye, of course,' he finally managed gruffly.

But deep down he wondered if she was ever coming back to him.

26

=====

THE CRYING SCENE

They went to the Portuguese restaurant where they had their memorable first night together. But somehow, everything was different. The waiters didn't seem so friendly, the music of the Spanish guitarist – which had been so magical the first time she had heard it – now sounded sad and mocking to Jude's ears. And some of the more well-to-do families had brought along young children to the restaurant, dampening the romantic atmosphere.

Colin tried to compensate for the awfulness of the situation by ordering generously. In addition to the feast they had enjoyed previously, he also requested an entire crab, cooked in a spicy Mediterranean sauce, a large plate of Portuguese paella and a jug of chilled mojito replete with large chunks of ice – somewhat superfluous on a cool Glasgow night. As the dishes piled up around them, Colin realised that he had over-ordered but Jude's sour mood had clouded his judgement. There was enough on their table for twice as many people. He had made the mistake with the jug of mojito too. Other women he had dated seemed to like the refreshing cocktail but in his flustered state he had forgotten that Jude didn't drink. Nevertheless, he poured them both a liberal serve into their tall glasses and even adorned Jude's with a sprig of mint. Then he heroically began tucking into their sumptuous repast.

'Try a little of the crab,' said Colin. 'It's delicious.'

Jude ignored both the food and drink. The only concession she made was to roll the sprig of mint in her drink back and forth between her thumb and forefinger.

'Colin, what are you saying? I don't understand any of this,' said Jude, distraught. 'You're an art dealer. How can you be mixed up with hardened criminals?'

When he had explained the situation to Jude on the phone the previous day, he had hoped to garner her sympathy by talking up the danger element of incurring the wrath of one of Glasgow's most notorious gangs – and his need for a quick exit. But Jude was having none of it. She had hounded him with teary recriminations on the phone and then again in the taxi on the way to the restaurant. She had wanted to go to his flat, but Colin persuaded her that this was not a good idea.

'I've been frantic with worry?' she added. 'Can't you try and reason with them.'

'These aren't the sort of people you reason with,' said Colin.

'But it was only a silly wee phone call anyway,' said Jude. 'Maybe someone was just playing a prank on you. You should tell the police.'

Once he had calmed down after the initial shock of the call, this had also occurred to Colin as the most likely explanation. But it was not in his best interest to admit that now. A clean getaway was required, not a drawn-out, messy separation.

He took a sip of his mojito and said nothing. It seemed to Jude there was an elusive quality to his departure, something she couldn't quite grasp.

'But don't you love me?'

'Of course I love you.'

'Then how can you leave me and go to America?'

Jude crushed the sprig of mint between her fingers and dropped it on the table.

'Darling, I'll be back as soon as this all blows over. I promise.'

'But I don't know when that will be. Take me with you,' she pleaded.

'Damn it, Jude. I said no!'

She recoiled a little and stared at him with shocked eyes. It was the first time he had raised his voice to her. But she refused to be cowed.

'How can you be so cruel, leaving me behind,' she said, 'when you know how much I love you?'

'What about your children?' said Colin. 'You can't leave them.'

Jude scoffed. 'That didn't bother you when you invited me to jump into your bed.'

'I need to travel light. I don't even have a place to stay over there yet,' said Colin.

'So this is what this is all about, getting away from me.'

'Don't be ridiculous. This is difficult for me too you know. Leaving my home town, leaving the woman I love.'

He put her hand over his and squeezed.

Jude looked into her lover's pained face. 'Of course. I'm being selfish,' she said. 'You must go. I would just die if anything happened to you. I just know that I'm going to miss you terribly...'

But a deep panic began to rise up within her. She suddenly felt a terrible certainty that she would never see him again. Her eyes began to swell with tears. There was a catch in her throat.

Colin watched with dismay. But he could do nothing She was entitled to her wretched scene. He realised she was going to cry. But as she was about to, a child at a nearby table began to bawl, a needy caterwauling. She looked down sullenly at her plate. Her tears had failed to materialise. Like a cloudburst, where the rain evaporates before it hits the ground.

27

=====

WHISKY AND BUDDY

'It's for the best really,' said Rita diplomatically. 'It's best for the children. And they need their father.'

Rita, who had egged Jude on and lived vicariously through the affair, had now changed sympathies – in line with the evolving situation of her friend's tumultuous romance.

Jude had the flat to herself. Jimmy had taken the children to their gran's but she had declined, feigning a bad migraine. But it was only a partial lie. Her mind was in tatters and she had the beginnings of what felt like a nasty headache. She was sitting in the armchair by the fire – the briquettes had burned down but the flat was overheated and stuffy. That's one of the problems with this accursed hovel, she thought. It's either freezing cold or boiling. There was, it seemed, no middle ground.

She had a bottle of whisky in one hand and the phone in the other. Needing comfort, she had turned to her best pal. She needed to talk to someone. The hurt and the loneliness were unbearable.

'It was just the most awful thing,' said Jude. 'After dinner, he just gave me a hug and a wee peck on the cheek. And then sent me on my way – like a common whore. He didn't even want me to see him off at the dock.'

'Och come on Jude, stop talking nonsense,' said Rita. 'You know he loves you. Have you heard from him yet?'

'His ship's supposed to arrive in New York tomorrow,' she said with a sniffle. 'But the funny thing is, I have this sense of dread. I'm not even sure if he's going to try and contact me.' Jude began to blubber quietly down the phone.

'That's the way,' said Rita, 'have a good cry now. Get it all off your chest.'

'I didn't mean to dump this on you,' said Jude.

'Don't be daft. What are friends for?'

Jude endeavoured to compose herself. She wiped her face with her handkerchief.

'Don't worry,' said Rita in a soothing voice. 'It'll all turn out for the best. You'll see.'

Although like a true friend, who had ringside seats to her disintegrating marriage, Jude suspected it was not what Rita really thought.

After Jude finally convinced Rita that she wouldn't do anything silly, the pair rang off – promising to meet for a cup of tea and a chat the next day. Left to her own devices, Jude clumsily unscrewed the cap from the bottle of whisky and took a mouthful. She winced at the taste of the vile liquid and the burning sensation as it went down her throat. While she disliked alcohol, she despised straight liquor worst of all, whisky in particular. She knew that she shouldn't be drinking, that in her it would only make things worse. But tonight she needed oblivion. And she was going to have it at any cost. She thought briefly of the sleeping pills on her bedside table and the relief they could bring. Perhaps she could just keep taking them one after another until there was no more hurt … just like Marilyn Monroe. Crazy thoughts! She recoiled at the idea. Better stay well away from those pills tonight, she told herself.

So she sat by the fireside, with her legs dangling over the upholstered arm of the chair, the fire warming the soles of her feet. She sang along quietly to show tunes on the radio, cradling the bottle of whisky in her arms.

It was Glenmorangie. Her husband always kept a bottle of the stuff on hand for guests and the like. But it seemed, to Jude, to be the same bottle of whisky. Constantly replenishing itself, a reminder of the failure of their life in Tain. But the whisky was giving her solace now. Better than the alternative in the bedroom. The pills of eternal sleep.

She wondered when the others would return. Soon, she hoped. She no longer trusted herself. They usually went to her mother's for tea on Sunday night but she was in no state to confront her, so Jimmy had taken the children to Granny Baxter's instead. Granny Baxter. So called to differentiate from the kids' other grandmother. Her mother. Who she knew would secretly revel in the sudden departure of her lover, if she had only known. Who she would never tell, of course. Jude could just imagine the massive guilt trip her mother would lay on her daughter if she ever did find out. No doubt she would have predicted the end of the affair. She could hear her mother's voice ringing in her ears. 'Who would want you?' her mother spat, like a venomous viper. 'You, who was such a stupid, ugly, unwanted child. And now you're a stupid, unwanted adult!'

Jude's mind drifted to the pills in the bedroom again. She shuddered at the thought. She tried to rid herself of the idea. Knowing that in her fragile state, anything was possible, that tonight she might just go over the edge.

The fumes of the spirit from the bottle rose up to her nostrils, reviving her a little. She'd only had three mouthfuls but she already felt drunk. There was a sudden sound of joy from the radio – a bright opening refrain. She recognised it as a Buddy Holly song, one of her favourites. She sang along with it – providing a perfect harmony to Holly's sweet lament – tears streaming down her cheeks while she cradled the bottle of whisky in her arms. The orchestral arrangement of the song tugged at her own heartstrings. She pictured the love of her life standing at the railing of a ship, gazing upon the wonder of the Statue of Liberty as the port and skyscrapers loomed on the horizon.

Jude realised she was sweating. She had been close to the fire for too long. With some effort, she rose from the armchair. She put the bottle of whisky on the table and walked over to the living room window overlooking the street. She peered out into the still night, streetlights shrouded in fog. She opened the window, letting in a flood of cold, fresh air. It was met with a flood of nausea. She suddenly felt very queasy. The taste of salt rose in her mouth and she knew she was going to be sick. She made it to the bathroom, just in time to vomit a good measure of Tain's finest single malt into the sink.

28

=====

NEW YORK, NEW YORK

Colin stepped out of his apartment building into crisp, late autumn sunshine. The sky a blue dome. Business, as they say, was good. True that he wasn't making big bucks (as the Americans liked to call it) yet but then he was only just getting established, building a reputation. But already he could see that the volume and size of the art deals in New York made Glasgow look positively provincial.

He thought of Jude now and again with a pang of regret. But really, he reflected, could it have ever worked out? Especially with all those children. Billy alone was bad enough – such a lippy little upstart. Much as he felt affection for Jude, spending time with other people's offspring – as he would have inevitably been pressed to do – was not high on Colin's list of priorities. No, it had all definitely turned out for the best.

He hailed a cab and headed uptown for a meeting. Everything here seemed bigger and bolder, even down to the bright yellow taxis. Colin had an appointment with a Mister Shroff at a well-to-do hotel. He pictured a rich Jewish industrialist who was making a fortune in the post-war American boom and was now looking to expand his collection of master artworks, as a way to do justice to his burgeoning wealth. Just Colin's kind of client.

The thought put Colin in a good mood. He was whistling Johnny Cash's *Ring of Fire* in the elevator on the way up to the rendezvous. But as soon as he entered the hotel room he knew something was wrong – there wasn't a venerable gentleman in sight.

'Where's Mister Shroff?' he asked, feeling his voice rise in a panicky falsetto.

Colin heard the door click shut behind him.

'He won't be joining us I'm afraid,' said one of the three men facing him. 'Let's just say he's been unavoidably detained. Sorry about that.' Colin suddenly realised there was no Mister Shroff and he felt a cold chill in the pit of his stomach. The accent was undeniably Glaswegian, Colin thought dully. But it did nothing to instil cheery thoughts of home.

'But we wouldn't want to waste this opportunity,' the man continued. 'Wee Alec is keen to discuss something with you.'

Colin looked around the suite, as if expecting to suddenly see a sinister figure materialise from the shadows.

'He won't be gracing us with his presence today. Travel doesn't agree with him.'

'Look,' said Colin, trying to keep his voice calm. 'Just get him on the phone. Let me talk to him.'

The man took a pair of black leather gloves from his overcoat and slowly put them on, making sure each finger fit snugly.

'No need to worry handsome,' said the man, clocking the startled look in Colin's eyes.

'There's been a terrible misunderstanding.'

'Aye, well you've got that right. No hard feelings, eh? We've even got a wee present for you.'

'Do you want money?' said Colin. 'I can get you money.'

The man shook his head sadly and reached into his pocket.

'Oh God. Just let me go,' Colin pleaded.

'You see, things is, we wouldn't want people back in Glasgow thinking Wee Alec's gone soft. It's just business you understand,' he said with a tight-lipped smile, only it wasn't actually a smile.

Colin felt a shiver of ice go through him.

The other men came forward and expertly pushed Colin down with a pillow, lowering him into a prone position. The hitman drew a gun from inside his overcoat. Colin watched it with bulging eyes.

'See this? This is a Beretta. I'm afraid we couldn't get a Scottish pistol at such short notice. But given your predilection for running away, maybe you prefer Italian anyway,' he said, as he pushed the gun into the pillow.

As Colin hunched in the corner, the hitman put three bullets into his cowering hide. Then he moved the pillow up to Colin's face and fired one final shot.

=====

29

THE POLIS 2

'You've got some explaining to do James Baxter.'

'What's this all about?'

'I'll ask the questions if you don't mind.'

There was no sign of his alcohol-infused mug of coffee. Perhaps Superintendent Middlemiss was having a less stressful day. He simply sat with his hands clasped in front of him on his desk, staring sternly at the man seated opposite him.

'Would you happen to know the whereabouts of a certain Colin McAllister?' said the police officer.

Baxter shook his head and looked back at the superintendent.

'We're helping the New York Police Department with their enquiries. Doing our bit for transatlantic relations, you might say.'

There were two sharp raps on the door and a constable entered the room with a pot of tea adorned in a colourful woollen cosy and crockery on a tray. The ensemble rattled as he traversed the room and plonked it down on the desk.

'Your morning tea, Sir,' he said and left.

'As far as we can ascertain,' said Middlemiss, paying no heed to the interruption, 'Mister McAllister left Scotland on the fifteenth of September, with a one-way passage on board the *Orlando Bloom* bound for New York. Sometime around mid-October, he rented an apartment on the lower east side, quite a nice one apparently. And then he simply seems to have disappeared off the face of the Earth. Without a trace. We have reason to believe that Mister McAllister left Scotland owing a rather large debt. Can you shed any light on that?'

'I can't be of any help with that either,' said Baxter flatly.

'We were given the information by a Miss Sheila Donnelly, a former employee of Mister McAllister. Nice bit of stuff wouldn't you say?'

'I don't know. I've never met her,' said Baxter.

Middlemiss looked down at the fingernails of his right hand, as if the disappearance of a man was of only trifling importance.

'I suppose you might be wondering why we called you in for questioning.'

'I've got a bit of an idea. But I've not seen Mister McAllister for some time – at least three months, probably more,' volunteered Baxter. 'It's true I thought he was a pal for a while. But fair to say we've had our differences.'

'Difference, yes. I thought you might. Now,' the superintendent began, pointing a finger at Baxter, 'from what we can ascertain Mister McAllister and your wife became quite – shall we say – "chummy" in the months leading up to his sudden departure from Glasgow. It's been the talk of the Glasgow Repertory. Quite the scandal. You should keep that little wifey of yours on a short leash James Baxter,' said Middlemiss wagging a cautionary index finger.

Baxter's impassive façade crumbled a little as his personal life was brought up. He looked resentfully back at Middlemiss.

'Look,' continued the superintendent, 'I didn't ask you to come in here to try and embarrass you with unsubstantiated gossip. To be frank, I don't put much store in the testimony of these theatre types, too prone to embellishment for mine. But your unique relationship with McAllister does make you a person of interest.'

'He's got nothing to do with me.'

The superintendent favoured Baxter with an intense stare. Moments ticked by. Baxter stared back and said nothing.

Middlemiss released his gaze and turned his attention to the tray on his desk. As he poured his tea, Baxter's eyes wandered around the room a little. The office appeared largely unchanged. The only difference Baxter spotted was that the shelf of Scottish literature behind the superintendent appeared broader than during his previous visit. *The Complete Works of Robert Burns* still occupied pride of place in the dead centre of the collection.

'A word of advice,' said the officer as he took a sip from his cup and grimaced. 'This is the second time I've seen you, following on from the unfortunate incident involving Mister Zogalla. One man missing, the other dead. Both connected to you. How do you explain that?'

Baxter shrugged. 'I really couldn't say. I just seem to have been caught up in an unfortunate series of events.'

'A victim of circumstance, is that it?'

'I'd say so.'

'Once here is bad luck, twice is a coincidence. Three times? Well… let's just say I hope not to see you here again. OK?'

'I'll make sure of it superintendent.'

'Good. Good,' said Middlemiss, drumming his fingers on the table as if wondering what to do next. 'Would you care for a cup of tea? The boys have just brewed a pot. It's a bit peely-wally mind. I keep telling them they need to put three spoonfuls' of tea in the pot, not two. Honestly, good help is so hard to find. You know how it is.'

'Oh aye', said Baxter without any idea how it was.

'How about a ginger snap then?' said Middlemiss, proffering a plate of biscuits.

'I'm fine, really.'

'Suit yourself.'

The superintendent took a sip of his tea.

'I seem to recall you hail from Govan,' said Middlemiss. 'You're not a Third Lanark man are you by any chance?'

'I am actually.'

'Is that a fact? When I was a kid growing up in Govan I never missed a home game,' said Middlemiss.

'I take my boys to Cathkin to see Thirds every other week.'

'And what about last season. Incredible, eh?

'I've never seen anything like it,' enthused Baxter.

'I usually get dragged along to Parkhead these days by my section chief. But it's not got the same atmosphere as Cathkin.'

'Right enough.'

'Is that pub still there? That place on Crown Street. What was it called… the Hi Hi Bar?'

'Oh aye.'

'It was quite rowdy as I recall. What with it being across the street from the Gorbals and all.'

'Just high spirits mostly,' said Baxter. 'It's packed every Saturday night.'

'Well,' said the police officer with a clap of his hands, his reminiscing seeming to have brightened his mood considerably.

'I think that concludes our business here for today. Let's just put your involvement in these two unsavoury incidents down to a matter of coincidence. I don't expect to see you here again. Although...'

Baxter cocked a wary eye in the superintendent's direction.

'...it seems a shame to miss an opportunity to have a chat about Scotland's greatest poet. It's not every day in this place we get someone who appreciates fine literature.'

Baxter cast an involuntary glance up at the Rabbie Burns almanac. For one horrifying moment, Baxter thought that Middlemiss was about to pluck the weighty tome from the shelf and break into a spirited rendition of Rabbie Burns *To a Mouse* – but he was mercifully spared.

'Tell you what,' said Middlemiss, 'why don't we catch up for a pint at the Hi Hi Bar sometime? Sort of relive old times. We can even swap stories about our favourite Rabbie Burns' poems.'

'Sounds great,' said Baxter as he began to rise from his chair.

'Just give me a week or so to clear my desk of a few cases that are dragging on. I'll be in touch. That's a promise.'

'I can hardly wait. Well, I'll be off then,' said Baxter, as he made a beeline for the door.

30

=====

CLOSURE

Blast and damn! The car won't start. The starter's turning over okay. Perhaps I've flooded the engine. I force myself to stay calm. Now is not the time to lose my composure. I tell myself to wait two minutes and then try the ignition again. I suppose I could have posted the vial. But what if they lost it? I don't really trust the Australian postal service. I don't want to leave anything to chance.

Outside, I can hear the wind buffeting the makeshift garage. The corrugated iron roof creaks with the force. I take the vial out of my inside pocket and carefully unwrap it. I roll it over and read the inscription on the small white sticker affixed to the underside of the vial. Written in a small, italicised font: *Monash Genetics Lab, 466 Centre Rd, Clayton, Victoria, 3168*. I double check it to make sure I have the right address.

I don't want to go into how this purloined DNA sample came into my possession, but it is not an act I am particularly proud of. Suffice it to say a sibling somewhat more elderly and infirm – and less compos mentis – than I was fleeced of the very essence of life itself. It's amazing how much information you can glean from a hair follicle sample from a brush or an inner-mouth skin sample from a toothbrush. Was I a full-blooded relative to my sibling or just a lowly half-blood? Could I achieve some crystal-clear clarity from the murky waters of my own origin? The catalyst for my failings? And a lifetime of feeling on the outer. Excluded. I could scream and shout, but I could never get in.

It's a least a forty-minute drive to Clayton, traffic permitting, and I want to make sure I get there with plenty of time to spare. Time to seal the deal, or in my case unseal the deal, and for the vial to spill its secrets.

It's time for closure.

But first I have to drive. Impatience gets the better of me and I turn the ignition key. The engine chokes and splutters and rumbles to a start. Thick grey smoke billows out of the exhaust pipe. I give a couple of pumps of the accelerator to clear out the cobwebs and the engine roars, briefly drowning out the pounding of the wind. The garage begins to cloud with exhaust fumes, filling with lead particulates and carbon monoxide. Better get out of here before I asphyxiate myself.

I scrape the side of the car against the side fence as I back out of the driveway Thirty years ago my car was a brand-spanking-new Toyota Corolla, gleaming white. Now it's a jalopy. I don't bother to get out to inspect the damage to the fence or the vehicle. Okay, so my eyesight is failing and my spatial orientation isn't what it was. I know the new law from VicRoads says you're supposed to re-sit the drivers licence test after you have been prescribed glasses (I got my first five years ago) to prove that you're still capable of driving. But so what – who the hell is going to make me? Try and catch me fuckers!

I've driven over the Westgate Bridge. And am now heading in a northerly direction along the Esplanade. I realise I've been drifting. I've been driving aimlessly along the St Kilda foreshore and I've missed my turn off to Clayton. I'm going to have to backtrack. It's hot in this wreck of a car. The air-con doesn't work and smoke continues to billow out of the exhaust. If a copper cruises past now, I could have some explaining to do. A rivulet of sweat runs down my forehead into my eye, generating a little sting.

The wind has lessened here. Perhaps beaten back by the sea breeze rolling in from Port Phillip Bay. There's only glorious sunshine. It's incredible, pouring out of a blazing February sky. Drenching everything. A summer's worth of sunshine in Glasgow couldn't match this.

'Get your exhaust fixed you bloody drongo!' cried out a bogan as he roars past in a whine of smoke and screeching tyres in a yellow Holden.

'Easy tiger,' I mutter under my breath.

I smile to myself; I won't allow my serenity to be ruffled by this vulgarian. I need to keep my equilibrium. The acrid stench of burnt rubber drifts through the open window and wafts up to my nostrils. But there's something else too. A wind gust circulates through the car, infused with the salty tang of the sea. It's fresh, like a slap. It brings with it a marked drop in temperature. More than a sea breeze, a cool change is sweeping across the bay, giving the city much-needed respite. I can feel the sweat on my face drying as a steady flow of chilled air sweeps through the overheated cabin.

I keep driving until I arrive at the turnoff for St Kilda Pier. I stop at the lights – left for the water, right for the way back to

Clayton and the genetics lab. I flick on my indicator. But for the first time since I have secured the vial I have doubts, aware of the power of the secret it holds. The answer so nearly in my grasp. I wonder if I should use the ammunition from the stolen gun in my hand. Especially as I am the one in the firing line of its existential bullet. I could simply fling the vial off the end of St Kilda pier and end this destructive obsession. But then maybe the cycle of not knowing would start up all over again. My torment to endure.

The vial is sitting in the passenger seat beside me, nestling precariously in the unravelled handkerchief. I must drive carefully to ensure it doesn't fall.

Like so many places in Melbourne, St Kilda is named after a place in Scotland. Saint Kilda. A windswept deserted island in the north of Scotland that fell on hard times. Not unlike Summerisle from *The Wicker Man* – a salutary tale if ever there was one. Perhaps an apt place for the vial, and its mystery, to meet a watery end. I have no intention of following the fate of the police sergeant in the movie who became the Wicker Man, an outsider whose foolishness and ignorance lead to his downfall in a sacrifice in a pagan festival. I want to be forearmed with knowledge. Or at least understanding. Maybe something like understanding is enough.

I remain stationary at the T junction. My indicator continues to flash. Hmm... I would have to think about that one. But not for long. The traffic light has turned green and cars have banked up behind me. Their owners, impatient with my vacillation, honk their horns. I move forward.

31

=====

NEW AUSTRALIANS

Baxter burst through the bedroom door brandishing a colourful brochure. He found Jude propped up on the bed reading. She had rarely seen him so animated, which put her immediately on guard. Baxter took off his jacket and draped it over a chair. She could tell from the scent of his sweat that he had been working out in his gym. But Jude sensed that was not what was creating his excitement.

'Where are the children?' he asked.

'They're away over at the Ross's,' said Jude. 'Playing cards.'

'Aren't they too young for cards?'

'They're probably only playing Snap. I don't think that's going to turn them into hardened gamblers just yet.'

Baxter moved towards his wife and sat down on the bed. 'I've got something to show you,' he said holding up the brochure. 'Look at this.'

'Hmm?' she said, raising her eye line above her book. The cover of the brochure featured a montage of images. Prominent was a large arched bridge over a breathtaking harbour. And kangaroos. Lots of kangaroos. Baxter began flicking through the brochure while Jude looked at the contents pensively over his shoulder.

'I want the sun,' said Baxter. 'It hardly ever shines here. There's too much gloom in Glasgow. It's always dark in our pokey wee flat. Och Jude, aren't you fed up with all this?'

Jude always thought a tan would improve her looks, but she wasn't ready to admit as much to her husband.

'I've heard Australia's always hot,' she protested, 'and it's full of snakes.'

'Just carry a big stick,' joked Baxter.

'And what about Gregor? He's just settling into high school here, making new pals.'

'He's young,' said Baxter. 'He'll make new pals in Australia.'

'But all our family's in Glasgow. My mother.'

'Your mother? I thought you'd be glad to get away from her. Anyway, other people are leaving too. Do you know the McCaskies have already booked their passage? They're leaving for Perth next month.'

'But it's such a long journey in those big boats.'

'Not anymore – the Australian government is starting to fly families out. All expenses paid. There's so many jobs, they haven't got the people to fill them.'

'Flying? Isn't that awful dangerous.'

'Don't be daft. But I haven't told you the best bit yet.'

'What's that?'

'There's this big firm. Commonwealth Aircraft Corporation. It's near Melbourne, someplace called Altona. They're crying out for gear cutters. They've got twenty positions available. Twenty! They posted an advert in the *Glasgow Herald*. And the pay is twice as much as I earn at Crockatt's.'

'That does sound grand,' Jude conceded. 'But are you sure you can do the job? It could be challenging.'

'They build military aircraft. Similar to the ones I worked on during the war. Plus, they offer training. It wouldn't take me long to get the hang of it.'

Baxter put the brochure down on the bed. He reached into his back pocket and took out a sheet of newspaper. He unfolded it and picked up a pen from the bedside table.

'Honestly,' Baxter continued, 'Australia sounds great. They've got all sorts of marvellous fruits – pineapples and watermelons and bananas. And people eat steak for their tea every day.'

'What's wrong with mince 'n' tatties?'

'You can have those too if you like. Christ Jude, you say I'm the one who never takes a chance. But here you're the one who's acting scared. C'mon let's do it. It'll be an adventure,' urged Baxter.

'I'm not scared,' said Jude. But in truth she was, at least a little – and taken aback by her husband's decisive behaviour.

'I'm just not sure. It seems like such a big step.'

'Suit yourself,' said Baxter irritably. He fell silent and turned his attention to the cryptic crossword.

Jude picked up the brochure and began idly flicking through it, staring wide-eyed at pictures of a bright, brash alien land. Her eyes wandered across to her husband, his back to her, head over his crossword. She breathed in the familiar scent of his sweat. She admired the play of muscles on his back, exposed through his white singlet. Whatever else Baxter's unknown father had given him, he had blessed him with a magnificent physique. And his boxing days might be behind him, but whatever else you could say about Jimmy Baxter, you couldn't call him a quitter. He still worked out. He still kept himself in shape. He still had plans.

'How about some skulduggery tonight?' she teased.

Jimmy groaned in exasperation and turned slightly away from her. Forgiving was one thing. Forgetting was something else. But the gleam in her eye remained. Only now it was more of a twinkle.

EPILOGUE

1964, Glasgow, Scotland...

The Baxter family were progressing along the walkway towards customs at Prestwick Airport. They had left their home in Govanhill for the last time and had caught a bus from the centre of Glasgow to the airport with all their worldly possessions in tow. They were booked to catch a one-way night flight on a BOAC VC10 jet airliner to Melbourne, Australia. Echoey announcements blared out importantly over the loudspeaker, announcing flight details to all parts of the globe.

There were six Baxters in total.

Trailing at the back was Hazel. Blossoming into her adolescence and struggling mightily as she carried a bag of her personal effects. It was weighed down with an impressive collection of LP records and singles – mostly Elvis Presley and The Beatles – that she simply had to take with her.

In front of Hazel were Jimmy and Jude, each carrying luggage, and in front of them the two eldest boys, Billy and Gregor, lugging a large trunk between them. It was a cumbersome piece of baggage of polished pine, secured by thick, brown leather straps, a sturdy padlock and with a metal handle at each end.

And out front was wee Bobby. The newest addition to the Baxter clan. Three years old and sporting a pair of thick-lensed Scottish National Health glasses to correct his lazy eye. Slung over his shoulder was his kindergarten school bag, full of crayons and loose pieces of paper and his favourite toy soldiers, to amuse himself on the long flight ahead. Relatively unencumbered and the most eager for the adventure ahead, he had dashed into the lead.

'Will it be hot in Australia?' Jude asked her husband. She had asked this and countless other questions many times but was seeking reassurance at this time of uncertainty. Usually so brave, she had become a bundle of nerves in the lead-up to the family's departure from Scotland. It was her reluctance that delayed their move to Australia by several years.

'It's winter there now,' said Jimmy.

'But it will still be warmer than Scotland, surely.'

'Aye, but everywhere's warmer than Scotland.'

'How long will be in America for?' said Billy, turning his head to ask his parents and bashing his knee into the corner of the wooden trunk in the process.

'We'll be stopping on the island of Hawaii for two days,' replied his father.

'That's braw,' said Billy. 'Will we have time to see the Statue of Liberty?'

'Don't be so bloody daft,' chimed in Gregor. 'That's in New York,'

'Language,' cautioned his mother.

'Cut it out you two,' said Jimmy. 'I don't want any fighting on the plane.'

'Wait for me!' called out Hazel from behind.

'For goodness sake Hazel. Will you hurry up? We're going to miss the flight at this rate,' said Jude. 'I don't know why on Earth you insisted on bringing all those records – I told you they've got records in Australia.'

But Hazel continued at her own pace. Wondering dreamily what the boys in Australia would be like. Would there be anyone as handsome as Paul McCartney? Beatlemania was in full swing in Britain but had anyone in Australia even *heard* of The Beatles.

Up front, wee Bobby slowed and then stopped dead in his tracks. Ahead, keen-eyed customs officials – men in smart blue uniforms – waited expectantly for the approaching families to present their travel papers for processing. Beyond that was the enormous immigration hall, filled with anxious, hopeful people. And beyond that planes on the tarmac, being refuelled for the voyages ahead.

It suddenly seemed like a very big world.